"My soul
and my delight..."

A thousand warning bells screamed in Maggie's mind. "Please—" she began.

"Shhh," George whispered, and the whisper turned into a kiss, gentle at first, then insistent, then fiery fierce, until lips bonded to lips, and there was no world beyond Castle Killashee. She did not resist. Could not. It was her own insistence he was meeting and matching, her own ferocity. She clung to him with all her might, as if to let go for an instant would be to lose him again, and forever....

Dear Reader,

Your enthusiastic reception of SECOND CHANCE
AT LOVE has inspired all of us who work on this
special romance line and we thank you.

Now there are *six* brand new, exciting SECOND
CHANCE AT LOVE romances for you each month.
We've doubled the number of love stories in our line
because so many readers like you asked us to. So, you
see, your opinions, your ideas, what you think, really
count! Feel free to drop me a note to let me know your
reactions to our stories.

Again, thanks for so warmly welcoming SECOND
CHANCE AT LOVE and, please, *do* let me hear
from *you*!

With every good wish,

Carolyn Nichols

Carolyn Nichols
SECOND CHANCE AT LOVE
The Berkley/Jove Publishing Group
200 Madison Avenue
New York, New York 10016

SHAMROCK SEASON
JENNIFER ROSE

A
SECOND CHANCE AT LOVE
BOOK

The author is indebted to Gail Wilson of Hollywood, who generously provided background information about video equipment and technique. Any errors are the author's own.

To Marnie Whelan,
shamrock friend.

chapter 1

"HAVE AN AFFAIR with George MacDonagh? Me? Are you crazy, Lou?"

Maggie Devlin's words tumbled out in an incredulous rush. She glared at the telephone receiver which had just relayed the appalling notion. "Give me credit for a little taste, will you?" she exploded. "He may be the most talented filmmaker since Hitchcock, but as a human being, forget it. The man is pure blarney, just like my Uncle Pat. Five minutes after we meet he'll be telling me my eyes are as green as shamrocks and my voice reminds him of the River Shannon on a summer morning. No thanks." She gave a puff of indignation, then added virtuously, "Anyway, I never get involved with the men I interview. It's unprofessional."

She regretted her words instantly, and decided to sign off before Lou Benjamin could ask with whom, exactly, she did get involved. Then she remembered the original purpose of her call. The man at the other end of the wire was the gardening editor of *Limelight*, the New York weekly magazine for which Maggie was a staff writer. She had called him to get advice about the tiny rooftop vegetable patch above her Greenwich Village apartment, only the conversation—like nearly every other conversation she'd had at *Limelight* since being assigned to interview George MacDonagh—had degenerated into a teasing session before she could get to the point. Now she described the alarming lacy edges on her Loosehead lettuce.

"Birds!" she exclaimed a moment later. "You're kidding me, Lou. Birds eat lettuce? I thought the little darlings lived on breadcrumbs and worms. What do I do, put up a scarecrow? I do? Really? Okay, I'll try it. Though I bet one of my neighbors spots it at night and calls the cops to report a burglar on the roof. Can't you just see the story in the *News?* I mean, who ever heard of a scarecrow in Manhattan?"

Maggie laughed, her good humor restored. Life in New York never stopped delivering surprises, that was for sure. She told Lou Benjamin he was an angel and added impetuously, by way of reward for heavenly deportment, "There's a screening of the new Clint Eastwood tonight. Want to go? Eight o'clock, sixteen hundred Broadway, fourth floor. Got to dash now. I'm meeting the great MacDonagh at Sardi's at one, and if I'm late he'll probably get stolen away by his groupies."

Hanging up, she sent a tiny sigh out into the world. Lou had been so pleased by her invitation, so enthusiastic about the prospect of seeing her later. If only she could come close to matching his excitement. She found him good company and admired his ability to elevate gardening to an art, but she hardly fluttered and flushed at the thought of sitting next to him in a darkened screening room, inventive hand-holder though he was. Then again, she didn't flutter and flush at the thought of close encounters with any man.

Once upon a time, before she'd learned the emotional cost of failing at marriage, Maggie had held a romantic view of divorce. Granted, divorce was always sad, that she knew. Still, viewed in the abstract, it had also seemed a rather exciting state—a public declaration of experience and availability that she imagined was matched by a private sizzle. She'd been divorced for nearly a year now and wasn't sure what she projected publicly. Privately, she was simply numb. She was having a harder and harder time even remembering what passion felt like. Sometimes she was tempted to put the lie to history and deny that passion had ever existed for her.

She looked at her watch. There was no time to weigh the imponderables of life. She pushed her fingers through her buoyant red hair, threw a notebook and felt-tip pen into her shoulder bag, and hurried out through the editorial offices of *Limelight*.

"Bring George back here," one of the research assistants called wistfully after her.

Maggie shook her head in wonderment. There it was again, the MacDonagh Effect. The entire female population of the United States seemed to have a crush on George MacDonagh. The young director had soared through the ranks of Hollywood to take hold of the public imagination in a way few directors ever did, let alone at age twenty-nine.

Fair enough—up to a point, Maggie thought. She believed in the *auteur* theory of film criticism— the director *was* the picture. It was about time the movie-going public gave the sort of adulation to a director they'd previously reserved for actors. And

George MacDonagh certainly deserved recognition for his fantastic talent, his unique blend of high poetics and low comedy.

But there was something a little suspect about his popularity—the flurry of appearances on TV talk shows, the posters and T-shirts bearing his carelessly handsome face. Maggie had the feeling that George MacDonagh was courting the public as vigorously as the public was courting him. She didn't suggest that the director skulk through the streets behind dark glasses, curtly refusing to talk to the press, but surely there was a middle ground between playing the recluse and selling oneself in the manner of the old-time starlets. It was unseemly for a director, an artist, to appear in ads for Irish whiskey, to have a slick piece of work like Harriet Mills as his press agent, sending around coy photos of her client in his four-seater California hot tub. Then again, Maggie thought grimly, George MacDonagh had surrendered his right to the title of artist. She regarded his current hit, *On the Make,* as nothing more than a big, glossy soap opera—and nothing less than a perversion of his talents. Why, oh why, had he sold out?

Well, Maggie Devlin would get to the bottom of the story. That was what the interview at Sardi's was going to be all about. Harriet Mills might be expecting yet another puff piece on her superstar client, but Maggie had something different in mind. The readers of *Limelight* were going to know the truth about George MacDonagh.

"Maggie! Fore!"

File folders flew as Maggie collided with Tracy Nichols, another *Limelight* staff writer and Maggie's roommate.

"Sorry, Tracy." Maggie stooped to help her friend retrieve scattered newspaper clippings. "I was daydreaming about what I'd like to do to George MacDonagh."

"I know what I'd like to do to him," Tracy sighed.

"Am I the only woman in America who doesn't want to go to bed with George MacDonagh?" an exasperated Maggie asked.

"I don't know why you don't." Tracy ticked off his virtues on her fingers. "He's brainy, single, hilarious, gorgeous, *and* one man you can't say isn't tall enough for you. He's even Irish."

"He was born in Brooklyn," Maggie snapped. "His parents were born in Brooklyn. He's further removed from Ireland than I am, unless you count all the Ballymacarbery whiskey he drinks. Anyway, he sold out his talent, which makes him singularly unappealing to me." She pirouetted around so that the wide skirt of her off-white Indian cotton dress flared. "How do I look?" she blurted out.

"Gorgeous, of course," Tracy replied, grinning knowingly at Maggie's abrupt change of mood. "Though how and why you walk around on those stilts is beyond me."

Maggie glanced down at her black patent leather sandals. "The heels are only two inches high," she protested. "If you'd spent your teen-age years waiting for all the boys to grow, you'd understand why I flaunt my height now."

"I'm just jealous," sighed the petite Tracy, brushing her sun-streaked blonde hair back off a face innocent of makeup. "I only really look at home in running shoes, and the best that can be said for my legs is that they can carry me the distance in the Marathon. Definitely not the George MacDonagh type. But you are, and you know it, and I bet you anything he comes on to you."

"He comes on to every woman," Maggie retorted.

Checking her watch, she added, "I'd better dash. Sorry to bite your head off. It's just—"

"Just the famous Devlin temper. Should be an interesting encounter. Have fun."

Maggie pushed the button to summon the elevator, then remembered her telephone conversation with *Limelight's* gardening editor.

"Tracy," she called out, "I talked to Lou, and he thinks it's birds who've been eating the lettuce, not insects."

"Birds! Whatever next?"

Maggie forgot about her garden and nearly everything else as she hurried along Forty-fifth Street and cut through Shubert Alley, the heart of the theater district. She took deep breaths in and out, the way she did when she was warming up for her daily half hour of yoga, then let her mind go limp. She tuned out the lunchtime crowd surging around her. That was better. Yes. She was refreshed now, ready to focus. She was ready, she thought cheerfully, to go for the kill.

She exchanged greetings with the doorman at the maroon canopied entrance to Sardi's restaurant, the festive gathering place that was as much a Broadway institution as greasepaint. The restaurant was jammed to the walls, she noted with dismay. Of course. Today was Wednesday, matinee day, and lunch at Sardi's was a must for those who wanted to see and be seen.

Maggie thought irritably that she didn't know why she had let Harriet Mills insist on a Wednesday lunchtime interview at Sardi's. Not that she would have to wait for a table. As a staff writer for one of the most influential New York weeklies, Maggie always commanded the desirable table thirty-four. But her interview with George MacDonagh would be interrupted by a parade of people, ordinarily possessed of better manners, who wouldn't be able to resist stopping at the table and gushing, "Oh, Mr. MacDonagh, I never miss one of your pictures. Would you mind signing on this napkin? It's not for me, of course, I wouldn't dream . . . It's for my daughter, she'll be thrilled to pieces."

Which exactly explained, Maggie thought with further irritation, why she was at Sardi's at one o'clock on this glorious Wednesday late in May. George MacDonagh probably cried himself to sleep at night if he'd gone the whole day without signing an autograph.

"Hello, Miss Devlin," the maître d' greeted her warmly.

"Hello, Albert. Gads, what a crowd. How do you manage to stay so serene? Have the rest of my party arrived yet?"

"Miss Mills called a few minutes ago. She and Mr. MacDonagh have been detained. Something about an overseas telephone call that finally came through. Her apologies, and they'll be here at one-fifteen."

Maggie made a face. The lateness was typical of Harriet Mills's game-playing.

"I'll dash upstairs, Albert," she said, "then come down and console myself with a Heineken."

"Good. Your table is ready when you are."

Maggie turned and walked up the steps to the second floor, then hesitated. Around to her right was a long, curved bar, presided over at this time of day by a bartender she considered one of the most charming men she'd ever met. But a deluge of painful associations also awaited her at that bar. She decided to forego the pleasures of a chat with Ivan Dimitri, and went straight into the powder room.

Maggie looked at herself in a mirror surrounded by lights like those in theatrical dressing rooms. Back in high school, after a brief fling with the drama club, she had realized she was more interested in writing for or about the theater than in being on stage. But looking at herself in the mirror at Sardi's was always strangely exciting—as if she were, in fact, about to step out into the limelight.

"Ham," she scolded herself, as she fluffed out her glossy red hair. "Egomaniac," she added, as she unabashedly admired the dusting of freckles across her patrician nose. How she'd loathed those freckles as a girl—until she'd come across some close-up photographs of the much-freckled Katharine Hepburn.

Blushing, she dropped the curtain on her performance as a frenzied woman in a seersucker suit burst into the room and all but accosted her.

"I don't believe it," the woman moaned loudly. "Do you by any chance have a safety pin? I've just snapped my— Oh, dear."

Maggie stifled a giggle. She wasn't sure what an "oh, dear" was, but she was certain it was something she wouldn't be caught dead wearing herself.

"I'm sorry, I don't," she told the woman. "The attendant's usually here on Wednesdays, and she would have one, but that doesn't help you much, does it? Why don't you ask the hatcheck woman downstairs?"

"I don't dare go downstairs," the woman moaned. She grabbed anxiously at various parts of her hefty anatomy.

According to Maggie's watch it was only seven after one. "I'll go ask the upstairs bartender," she told the woman. "Wait right here."

"You're a doll." The woman sank gratefully onto the tweed divan next to the full-length mirror. "Don't I know your face? Aren't you somebody?"

Maggie bit back the obvious retort and headed out past the stairway to the curving mahogany bar where Ivan Dimitri had shaken and poured for thirty years.

"Maggie!" Ivan threw open his arms.

She pushed aside a bar stool and leaned over to

kiss his cheek. "Darling Ivan. You're well?"

"The better for seeing you. You look glorious."
He hesitated a moment then added, "The professor
was in here the other day."

Maggie stiffened, then sighed. "Oh?" she finally
said. "How was he?"

"He looked very lonely."

"Oh, Ivan." Maggie dearly loved the courtly dark-
haired bartender, but she did wish he'd stop trying to
revive the world's deadest marriage. How to tell him
without hurting him? He only meant well. He adored
Maggie and greatly admired her former husband, John
Venable, the noted professor of theater history. Some
of Maggie and John's happiest hours had been logged
over drinks at Ivan's bar, and Ivan still couldn't accept
that the rest of their life had not been merry.

Maggie tried once again. "You know, some drinks
just don't mix, Ivan. John is white wine, and I'm
beer, and never the twain shall meet." She smiled,
but in fact that trivial difference of taste had taken on
symbolic importance and become the source of endless tension. Her husband had thought it looked inele-
gant for Maggie to drink beer at bars. Never mind
that she sipped it from delicate stem glasses. Never
mind that when she was thirsty no other tipple could
slake her. Never mind—most important—that she
genuinely loved the taste of beer. And she had been
bored to tears by John's endless waxing lyrical about
this vintage of Sylvaner versus that bottling of
Gewürztraminer.

"Maggie, I didn't mean to upset your," Ivan said
contritely. "Sit. Let me give you a Heineken with
many, many rocks."

"First chance I get," Maggie promised Ivan and
herself, "but I'm doing an interview downstairs and
I have to dash. I came over to give you a kiss, and
to ask you, on behalf of a woman who will otherwise

be stranded forever in the ladies' room, if you have a safety pin."

Ivan reached under the bar and instantly produced two pins. "Two is better than one," he smiled.

Maggie waggled an admonishing finger at him, deposited another kiss on his cheek, and went back to the ladies' room.

"Thank you, thank you, dear," the seersucker woman breathed.

"You're welcome." Maggie turned to leave, deciding she really couldn't bear to know what the woman was going to do with the pins. But the woman wasn't through with Maggie.

"Are you here for the same reason I'm here?" she asked with a moist little giggle.

"I have no idea," Maggie answered, not hiding her impatience.

"I heard it on the radio. In the cab. One of those interviews, you know? Gil Gross, he always gets the best celebrities. I was on my way to Bloomingdale's to do a little shopping for my daughter, she's expecting a baby, her first, and she doesn't have so much as a jar of powder, she's sure Nature will provide, but I'd rather put my trust in Bloomie's, thank you— Anyway, when I heard on the cab radio that George MacDonagh was going to be at Sardi's, I told the driver, 'Forget Bloomingdale's, the baby won't be here for a month, what's the rush? Take me to Sardi's.' I thought *On the Make* was the funniest thing I ever saw, didn't you? My husband—"

"George MacDonagh announced on the radio that he was coming to Sardi's?" Maggie asked incredulously.

"That's right. Do you suppose he's meeting Genevieve Joyce for lunch? I read in the *Post* that she's dying to have him direct her. Just between you and me, her husband's crazy if he lets her get anywhere near George MacDonagh. He—"

Maggie didn't wait to hear the rest of the sentence. Color rising hotly in her cheeks, she marched down the stairs.

chapter 2

FOR DAYS SHE'D been looking at photographs of him as she prepared for the interview.

She'd seen shots of him grinning over a large wooden salad bowl heaped high with bean sprouts (part of a Sunday supplement article called *Hollywood Is Cooking Without Gas*). She'd seen glossies of him squinting into the California sun as he lolled in his hot tub. She'd seen him winking down at her from a Times Square billboard as he raised a Waterford crystal glass and toasted the world with Ballymacarbery Irish whiskey. She'd seen him on late-night talk shows, crossing and uncrossing his long blue-jeaned legs, creating instant limericks on any excuse, dropping into a dreadful brogue, and making irreverant comments about the news items of the day.

13

She'd grudgingly had to go along with the consensus—he was attractive. He was a kind of outsize leprechaun, all height and wiry thinness. He had pale blue eyes that seemed to see the jokes in things, and untamed dark hair that fell over his forehead in a shock and got mixed up with his collar (when he bothered to wear a shirt). With his upturned nose and dimpled chin, he looked like what her Uncle Pat, the professional Irishman, would proudly hail as a "right scarperer," an exalted mischief-maker. He looked to be a right Californian, too, part of the new breed who rode wild horses and then went home and meditated, who were both macho and liberated.

Check. Attractive. She'd conceded the point and gone on to other thoughts. Were a director's looks what mattered, after all? Had Alfred Hitchcock ever won a beauty contest?

Now, as he approached table thirty-four at Sardi's, exactly one-half hour late, Maggie Devlin had to concede that George MacDonagh was more than attractive—he was devastating. He was the once-in-a-life-time man who leveled a woman's emotional underpinnings just as a tornado could lay waste the sturdiest of cities.

She felt her lips part as he moved toward her, seemingly oblivious of the staring—no, gaping—women at the tables he passed. She felt pulses beating in places where pulses had no business beating. Her breath came from way inside her back, and hurt. Her thermostat fluttered wildly. Within seconds she was flaming, then freezing, then flaming again. For one terrifying moment she thought she'd been struck by some dreadful acute illness. No, not an illness. Dear God, no. Just desire, raw and base and utterly, swellingly sweet.

Instantly body and soul struggled to repel the sensations she was feeling. Desire gave way to a surge of fury at the young director. He had no business playing up his physical assets the way he did, loping long-leggedly toward her with that cocky grin on his merry, weathery face, assessing her like a casual connoisseur, as if she were the *plat du jour* on Sardi's menu. She felt a deeper surge of fury at herself for responding to him on some primitive level she couldn't control. Never mind that only an hour earlier she'd longed to feel herself in the grips of passion again. This excitement was tainted. She was falling for a packaged product, for a press agent's hype.

He moved in on her before Harriet Mills could make the proper introduction.

"Hey, Maggie Devlin," he said, with a gentle lilt that was just this side of a brogue. He fixed his pale blue eyes on her in one of those dead-level California guru gazes. Then the scarperer took over again, and the eyes twinkled.

Maggie gave him a cool New England "Hello." She held out a formal hand—and managed to knock her Heineken bottle into the ice-filled stem glass she'd just topped up, sending bottle, glass, beer, and ice skittering across the table and onto the red carpeted floor. Heads turned at nearby tables. A busboy came rushing over to change the wet tablecloth and clean up the mess underfoot. Maggie desperately tried to conjure a witticism, but her mind was suddenly as clumsy as her body.

George MacDonagh had no such problem. He puckered his lips, whistled up his muse, and, leaning over the table and looking down at Maggie, produced one of his famous instant limericks.

"There was a young woman named Maggie
"Who when she was off on a jag, she

"Knocked over drinks
"And indulged in high jinks,
"That astounding young woman named Maggie."

"Very clever," Maggie acknowledged grudgingly.

"Aren't I just?" George MacDonagh settled himself next to her and gave her arm a squeeze. "Never mind. No other lips should touch the glass you've drunk from. Throw them all away, I say." He planted an impish kiss on her cheek. "You're a nice sight on a spring day."

Maggie did not think of herself as stuffy. She lived in that ancient bastion of bohemianism, Greenwich Village. She talked to strangers on the streets. The elaborate manners of some of her former husband's academic friends had maddened her. Her present roommate was a self-described swinger. But the instant intimacy that George MacDonagh projected— what she tagged as his California style—grated on her.

Now his expensive blue-jeaned thigh was pressing against her thigh. The thin cotton of her dress was no barrier at all. Her skin stung where they made contact. She wriggled away without making any attempt to disguise what she was doing.

"This damn table, Maggie," Harriet Mills cried to cover the moment. "I don't know why you like this corner. Hardly room to breathe. Not to mention how obscure it is. Strictly for a married man and his mistress, I say." She waved a pudgy, imperious hand. "Let me get Albert to move us out of Siberia."

"We'll stay right here," Maggie said firmly. "Don't worry. George's groupies will manage to find him. Especially," she added darkly, "since he announced his whereabouts over the radio. Are they lining up ten-deep outside?"

"Was this supposed to be a secret rendezvous?"

George made suggestive moves with his broad Irish eyebrows. "Not that I'd mind having one with you, Emerald Eyes. I bet you're fun when you relax." He casually reached under Maggie's hair to gauge the tension in the back of her neck. "Just as I thought. Tight as a high wire. You ever have a shiatsu massage? I'd love to get my hands on your body."

"George!" Harriet Mills exclaimed with more giggle than scold in her voice, sounding very much the shocked but secretly pleased mother. "Ah, there you are," she said, as the waiter appeared with a fresh Heineken. "Maggie, how do you drink beer and stay so thin? I suppose I should have a Perrier." The press agent was a study in circles, from her gray curls down to her plump ankles. "But what do I have to be thin for? I hate mineral water. Makes me belch. I'll have a very dry martini, straight up, hold the vegies."

George ordered a Ballymacarbery Irish whiskey, neat. He looked at Maggie. "Sure, and I couldn't drink to such a grand redhead with anything less," he declared, in his broadest brogue.

Maggie got out her notebook and pen and slapped them down on the table. She pretended to mull.

"Redheads. Redheads. Did I overlook a fondness for redheads when I was reading the clips on you? Let me see. Linda Lessing is a brunette." Linda Lessing was the star of *On the Make* and, according to the columns, a rather close friend of the director's. "Micki Brooks is a blonde," naming a California pop star who'd hit the top of the charts with a torch song called *George's House*. "So is Elizabeth Barry." Elizabeth was a free-lance writer whom Maggie knew slightly. She had written a graphic magazine article about her affair with George. Maggie shook her head as if in sorrow. "No known preference for redheads. Definitely not."

"Maybe it's time I expanded my tastes," George

MacDonagh said. His pale eyes looked amused.

"Maybe it's time you got some taste, period," Maggie returned sweetly.

"Oh, George," Harriet tsk-tsked. "She has you cold."

"No," grinning, "she has me hot."

"Too much!" Harriet cried, all but toppling onto the table with mirth. "Maggie, did you ever meet such a naughty man?"

"Never," Maggie declared gravely, "and I'm just sorry I'm not on assignment for one of the scandal sheets. I'm afraid the readers of *Limelight* don't give a damn about George MacDonagh's sex life. What they want to know is this: Why did the most talented director in America turn his back on his gifts and go Hollywood? Your god used to be creativity. Is it money now? Why are you playing the bi-coastal buffoon, chatting it up on talk shows and planting items in the gossip columns instead of hiding away in the woods the way you used to and working on a new script?"

She opened her notebook. She looked at George and noted with satisfaction that the grin had finally disappeared. She aimed her final punch. "I get the terrible feeling you've decided to throw all your creative energies into inventing yourself, selling yourself. Granted, George MacDonagh is interesting. But is he art?"

"If ever a man needed a drink!" George declared, as the waiter returned with his Ballymacarbery whiskey and Harriet Mills's naked martini. George raised his glass and gravely clinked it against the goblet of beer and ice which Maggie held in her hand. The clink reverberated through Maggie's body, as though flesh had nudged flesh instead of glass touching glass. Something about the way George's pale blue eyes wandered restlessly over her face, like twin bees searching out honey in a clover field, made her think that he had meant her to feel touched. For one wild instant she simply wanted to yell, "Yes!" She had to look away to steel herself to her purpose as the director said to Harriet, "You promised me she was going to be a real pussycat. What are the tigers going to ask me?"

"You're a snob, Maggie, that's your trouble," Harriet pronounced over her martini. "You want George to be the property of a few artsy types in Greenwich Village. You probably loved going to the Bleecker Street Cinema on a rainy Thursday midnight to see his pictures. You can't bear seeing people waiting outside the biggest house on Broadway to get into *On the Make*."

"That doesn't mean I can't bear the idea of George MacDonagh being mass-market culture," Maggie returned. "I happen to believe that, given a choice, the public prefers great pictures to junk."

"Wait a minute." The director held up his hand. *"The New York Times* called *On the Make* a romantic comedy in the great tradition, and if *The Times* said it, it must be true." His tone joked; his look challenged.

"I read that review, too," Maggie said, "and I couldn't believe that the reviewer and I had seen the same movie in the same screening room on the same night. But what he thought of it and I thought of it is not the point. What did you think of it, George? Did the creator of *Dublin Dreams* really like *On the Make?*"

He gave Maggie a dark look. "You liked *Dublin Dreams?* It lived up to your high standards?"

"I adored *Dublin Dreams*. It's my favorite of your films, one of my favorite movies ever made by anyone."

"That would be your favorite." George swallowed whiskey.

"I suppose you disown it now—"

"Did I say that?"

"Well, it's about really being Irish, isn't it, the good and the bad. And that's a far cry from making up blue limericks on a TV talk show and hawking Ballymacarbery whiskey. You—"

"Oh, *Dublin Dreams* is a dear little movie," Harriet Mills interrupted, "if you go in for those low-budget things. But it's just not in the same class with what he's done lately. I wouldn't be surprised if *On the Make* ran away with the Oscars."

"Is that what counts?" Maggie cried. "What I want to know is this. When you get around to making your next movie, George MacDonagh, assuming you ever get off the publicity circuit, what's it going to be? *Dublin Nights Revisited?* Or *Son of On the Make?*"

"Before he makes either one, I think we should all have lunch," Harriet Mills suggested nervously. She scanned her menu. "Why am I bothering to look? I'll have cannelloni. I can never pass it up."

"I'll have another Irish whiskey," George said. He gave Maggie a sour look. "Is this your patented interviewing technique? You bludgeon your victims with horrible accusations, drive them to drink, then worm all sorts of insidious quotes out of them when they don't know what they're saying? Fun."

Maggie flushed. "I'm sorry if you think I've been hostile. I respect—"

"Of course you do," Harriet soothed. "And I think you ought to be the first to know what George's next picture is going to be."

"Harriet—"

"George, believe me, I know what I'm doing. Why should *The Times* and *Variety* get all the scoops? Let *Limelight* break the story. I bet it's worth the cover."

"I can't guarantee it," Maggie said, "but I think Shakespeare would have to rise from the grave to knock it off the cover."

"But, Harriet—"

"Hush, George. She'll love it. She's young. What are you, dear, twenty-three?"

"Twenty-four."

"Exactly. George," she said in ringing tones, "is going to make a rock musical, the biggest rock musical ever. That was what the phone call was about that delayed us. We were talking to Eric Knightsbridge in London. He's going to star. Don't you think he's just too divine?"

"A rock musical?" Maggie echoed.

"*The* rock musical," Harriet said.

"But there are a dozen competent directors who can turn out a good rock musical." Maggie looked at George. His scarperer's face was wrought with some stormy emotion she couldn't fathom. "You're in a position of total strength," she said. "You can call the shots. If you wanted to make *Hamlet* with a cast of kangaroos, you could get the backing. Do you really *want* to make a rock musical? You need a second house in Malibu? Your own jet?"

George pushed back the table and stood up. All traces of the jaunty limericist had vanished.

"Damn it, I don't have to take this," he said, in a low, cold voice, "and I won't take it." He looked thunderbolts at Maggie. "Write whatever you want about me. I don't care."

Harriet was on her feet, too, catching at his sleeve, pleading with him, with both of them.

"George! Maggie! You bad children! This is ridiculous! In all my years in the business I never—"

She was interrupted by the screeching arrival at their table of the woman whom Maggie had rescued with safety pins.

"But, my dear!" The woman reproached Maggie with great familiarity, as if they were old friends. "You didn't tell me you were having lunch with *him!*"

She held out both her hands to George MacDonagh. "I'm Charlotte Prentiss from Bronxville, and I just want you to know that—"

The man who loved his public brushed rudely past her and strode out through the restaurant.

chapter 3

It took Maggie ten minutes to take care of the bill at Sardi's (a nearly apoplectic Harriet Mills tried desperately to pick up the check, but *Limelight* had a firm rule about never letting press agents pay for anything). It took Maggie another ten minutes to get back to her desk. It took her just under two hours to pound out her story on George MacDonagh. It took two minutes to walk the story down the hall to Ben Harris, editor-in-chief of *Limelight*. It took fifteen minutes to get a call from Ben summoning her back to his office.

"It's going to be the cover!" Maggie thought jubilantly, all but skipping away from her desk.

She was certain that the article on George MacDonagh was the very best piece she had ever written, maybe one of the best pieces any reporter had written for *Limelight*...for any magazine. The entertainment industry—the whole city—was going to be talking about her portrait of George MacDonagh for weeks to come. She even had visions of a Pulitzer Prize. She might not have written about the most earth-shattering subject, but she'd told the truth, told it straight out, no apologies, no window dressing. And that was the most valuable act a reporter could perform, whether covering a war or a restaurant or something in between.

"Sit down, kid," Ben Harris said, as she walked into his office. He was short, balding, somewhere past retirement age, one of the smartest and kindest people Maggie had ever met—and probably the only man in New York City who could get away with calling her "kid."

"Well?" she asked eagerly, dropping into the worn leather armchair across from his desk.

"It's brilliant," he said. "The best prose that's come across this desk in years. I'm not going to run it."

She just stared. He had to be joking. She waited to see his grin, his dear lopsided grin. No grin appeared. Ben picked a battered old ruin of a cigar out of an ashtray and chomped down on it.

"I don't understand," Maggie said.

"It's brilliant, but it's not reporting. It reads like some kind of vendetta." Ben took the cigar out of his mouth and flung it halfway across the room to a large metal wastebasket. It landed in the basket. Ben's cigars always landed in the basket. "What did this guy do?" he asked Maggie. "Love you and leave you?"

"Nothing of the sort! Ben! How could you?"

"Sorry, kid. But this piece isn't like you. It's cruel."

"Cruel?" Maggie protested. "You know who's cruel? The critics who are falling all over themselves to praise *On the Make* because they're afraid people will think they're elitist if they don't. They're being cruel to the movie-going public, cruel to George MacDonagh, and traitors to their profession."

"Maggie, girl. Whoa. You're going way overboard here. There are critics in this town who love to hate a movie, our own Spencer White among them. Now if he—"

"That's why you're spiking the piece," Maggie interrupted. "Because it doesn't jibe with what Spencer said in his review." She crossed her arms and glared at her editor, as if daring him to refute her.

"Nonsense," Ben scoffed. "Anyway, you didn't just pan a movie in your piece, you panned a human being. Aside from the question of taste, I'm not sure your piece isn't ripe for a lawsuit. Even if I passed it, I bet out lawyers would have a screaming fit over it."

"Why don't you get Harriet Mills to write your piece about George MacDonagh?" Maggie got to her feet. "That would probably suit your standards for objective reporting."

"Sit down," Ben barked. He flipped open his humidor and got a fresh cigar. Maggie stood poised on the threshold of a dozen different moves, each more dramatic than the next, then quietly sat down. "Listen to me, Maggie, and listen to me good. Have I ever tried to water you down? No," as she shook her head, "I haven't. I hired you when you were just out of college, green as they come, because you had passionate opinions—off the wall, some of them, to my mind, but never faddish, never cheap."

"You hired me because I was Mrs. John Venable."

Ben gestured dismissively. "Come on, Maggie girl. Why the hell do you suppose I pushed you to use your maiden name for your by-line? Because you were an individual then, as much as you're an individual now. I was sorry to see the marriage bust up, sorry to see you hurt. But, frankly, kid, you're the better writer for being out from under John's influence. He may speak a dozen languages and have a doctorate to go with every one of them, but a person needs a rake and two pickaxes to get through his prose." He held out Maggie's manuscript. "This isn't worthy of you, Maggie. It's got the passion, but the passion's perverted. What do you say you give it another go? Sleep on it if you—"

His telephone rang. He grabbed at it.

"Harris," he snapped. "What? Who? Clive! How are you, you son of a gun?" He signaled Maggie to wait.

She sat numbly in her chair. Her article, her precious article, her passport to a Pulitzer, lay on Ben's blotter, where he'd dropped it. She looked around the office. The framed covers of old issues of *Limelight,* the unframed pictures of Ben's grandchildren, the never-quite-perfectly-clean venetian blinds, the ugly wastebasket where Ben pitched his used cigars—it was all very familiar, very dear. Her throat felt lumpy and scratchy. There was suddenly too much emotion to swallow.

Ben finished his telephone conversation. He picked Maggie's article back up and held it out to her. "So what do you say, kid? You want to run it through the typewriter again?"

"If I say no?"

"We can live without a piece on George Mac-Donagh." He shrugged. "Hammer fallery's doing a show of William Horton. I can go with that for the cover. 'American Impressionist Comes Home.' Like it?"

"Sure. Fine. I've seen Horton's paintings. They're exciting. The only trouble is, Horton is dead, and the piece won't do him much good, even if he gets the cover. My piece might have saved an artist's life."

She stood up. "Ben, I love you. You've taught me—
I can't begin to calculate how much. I'm sure you
think you're doing the best thing for everybody, in-
cluding me, in not running this piece. But I can't live
with it. There's something fundamental at stake here."
She managed a small, sad smile. "I guess I'm trying
to find the words to say, 'I quit.'"

She picked up her article, made an airplane of it,
and sent it sailing across the room to Ben's big metal
cemetary for dead cigars.

chapter 4

CLEANING OUT A desk after quitting a job was almost
as heartwrenching an act, Maggie thought dismally,
as cleaning out a home after the breakup of a marriage.

Every object brought with it a wave of memory
and emotions, from the stubs of tickets for opening
nights on Broadway to her battered copy of the
writer's bible, *Elements of Style*, to the take-out menus
from the Japanese sushi restaurant down the block,
to a telegram she'd long since committed to heart but
had never been able to throw away.

It read: "Talent tells by any name. Venable loves
Devlin."

Those had been the great days. The marriage brand-
new and looking full of infinite promise, Maggie's
career no less so, and the two charmingly intertwined.

The telegram from her then-husband had followed publication of her first story in *Limelight,* based on an interview with an actress known the world over for her allergy to the press. John Venable had originally introduced the two women at a small party of theater people, assuring the actress that Maggie was there in her "civilian" capacity, not as reporter. The aging star had been disarmed by Maggie's youth and exuberance and had startled everyone by virtually demanding that Maggie interview her—handing her what would have been a real scoop for any reporter, and was a smash beginning for a cub's career.

Maggie fingered the much-creased telegram. The actress had made her final exit a few months ago; Maggie had written her obituary. The curtain had rung down on the marriage of Maggie Devlin and John Venable. And now Maggie had posted the closing notice on her career at *Limelight,* just when it was looking to be a long-run hit.

She crushed the telegram in her fist.

Tracy Nichols came running over to Maggie's desk, the embodiment of dismay. "Maggie! Whatever's going on? I just saw Ben, and he's in a state. He says you quit, and he couldn't talk you out of it, and that's the end of it."

Maggie shrugged and tried for a smile.

"But why?" Her blonde friend all but wept. She dropped onto Maggie's desk, right in the middle of the chaos.

"He spiked the George MacDonagh story," Maggie said.

"That's why you're quitting? Because you got the spike? Everyone gets the spike. It's like—" Tracy looked over the big editorial office, searching for a metaphor. Typewriters clacked around them. There was the sound of someone angrily jerking a piece of paper out of a machine and rolling in fresh paper. "It's like doctors losing patients. It happens to the best. You swallow hard and you go on."

Maggie sighed heavily. "I love Ben, and I admire him, but this story was spiked for the wrong reason."

"Give it a week," Tracy pleaded. "Ben is devastated. I'm devastated. You're throwing your career down the drain."

"Don't worry," Maggie said. "I'll get another job. I'll carry my share of the rent." Then, instantly, "I'm sorry, Tracy. I know that wasn't what you meant at all."

The two women were suddenly surrounded by other staff members as the rumor of Maggie's imminent departure filtered through the office. Already there were distortions.

"Is it true you're going to be the new movie reviewer for *Time?*" the assistant dance editor asked with undisguised envy. "Your ex pull some strings for you?"

Maggie laughed, then felt tears pool in her eyes. This was her family. She was going to miss these people.

She tried to cover her emotions by going back to work sorting the contents of her desk. There were treasures to take home and store in big envelopes at the top of her closet, junk to throw out, office property to leave behind. Where did some of this stuff come from? Amazing what people kept in their desks. The lid from a container of raspberry yoghurt—why on earth had she saved that? Into the basket. A brochure from the Irish Tourist Board. She paused, she felt a pang. It went into the basket. Even if she got another job right away, she wouldn't have three weeks of paid vacation in August. Good-bye, dreams of going to the Abbey Theatre in Dublin. Good-bye, dreams of biking through County Cork, staying in cozy little bed-and-breakfast places, conjuring the friendly ghosts of her ancestors.

When she'd finished cleaning her desk, she reached for the telephone and dialed Lou Benjamin, the gardening editor.

"Lou? Maggie. I'm afraid I have to disinvite you to that movie tonight. I think I've lost my screening room privileges. I just quit."

"I know! I heard thirty seconds ago. I was on my way down. Can I buy you a drink?"

Maggie smiled. That was Lou, all right. No probing questions, no lectures, just pure friendship. Well, almost pure.

"Thanks," she said, "but I want to go home and stand under a cold shower. For about a week."

"This isn't the end, is it?" Lou pleaded. "We can still have lunch, can't we? For you, I'd even go back to Greenwich Village, though I swore I'd never set foot south of Fourteenth Street again. I ought to have a look at that garden of yours, anyway. I bet your lettuce needs thinning. I know your type, too softhearted to kill anything living. I bet you even hate to kill weeds."

"That's not the way Ben Harris feels about me," Maggie replied, vinegar in her voice. She gathered up her belongings, patted her desk, made her last round of farewells, and headed home.

chapter 5

TRACY NICHOLS HAD never been able to sell Maggie on the joys of jogging. To get up at dawn and huff around Washington Square Park, breathing in all that carbon monoxide—Maggie just couldn't buy it. Walking was something else. Sure, you breathed the same awful air, but you didn't pull it quite so vigorously into your lungs. Besides, walking got you somewhere. And if you walked from home to work and back again, as Maggie did nearly every day, you got an important extra benefit—escape from the crowded subways, the lumbering buses.

On this upsetting afternoon, Maggie longed to slink into a taxi and let it cart her weary body home. But the fatigue was emotional, not physical, she knew. The walk would make her feel better. And somehow it seemed important to stick to the routine, the ritual, this one last time. She looked at her watch. She tapped her toes. She gave herself forty-five minutes to walk the thirty-eight blocks—just under two miles—to her apartment on Sixth Avenue near Eleventh Street, a decent pace by New York City standards.

She'd considered the number of major intersections she would have to cross, the amount of human traffic on the sidewalks in the late afternoon, the heat of the day, and the height of her sandals. But she'd overlooked one variable. She'd forgotten she would pass by the huge billboard of George MacDonagh raising his glass of Ballymacarbery whiskey. Even if she'd remembered, she could scarcely have known how forcefully it would halt her, how long it would arrest her.

Maggie stood at the corner of Forty-third Street and Seventh Avenue staring up at the mesmerizing advertisement. Shock waves ran through her body. She'd always appreciated the poster as a clever example of magic-realism. Now, with the memory of George MacDonagh's face and presence so fresh in her mind, the poster positively spooked her. The pale blue eyes were alive, and looking down at her. The glass was reaching out to nudge her goblet of beer. The mouth was framing a teasing limerick with her name in it. Somehow the man in that poster knew that Maggie's body craved his body, and that the craving had tricked her into throwing her job away.

She finally forced herself to go on, almost at a run. She forced herself to focus on her surroundings as she cut down through the fashion district, past Madison Square Garden, through Chelsea with its interesting mix of manufacturers and a growing population of artist loft-dwellers.

Her love for the city gave her wings. Her parents and her two older sisters were hooked on Boston, but from the time she was in high school Maggie had dreamed of going to New York and being a writer. Four years at Barnard College had been the first step, and every subsequent hour had reinforced her feeling that it had been the right step. Neither George MacDonagh nor sudden unemployment could undo that feeling.

After the break-up of her marriage, her parents had urged her to return to Boston to make a new life for herself. Maggie loved her parents, and every reminder of John hurt for a while, but to have divorced New York as well would have been to die a double death. She had left the apartment up near Barnard and Columbia to John—it had never felt like her apartment, anyway—and moved down to the Village with Tracy. That was enough new life.

And if she wanted to keep that new life, she was going to have to act quickly, she realized now. New York was expensive, and she'd never been a great saver. She'd have to get another job right away.

She could borrow money, of course. She had lots of friends. She could lean on her family in a pinch. But borrowing was so messy. Being taken care of by other people was a kind of un-freedom. She'd hated the feeling of imbalance at the beginning of her marriage, when John was making decent money as a Columbia professor—and an author and lecturer as well—and she was a student, earning nothing. Oh, the joy of that first paycheck from *Limelight*. She'd blown nearly all of it on a weekend for the two of them at the fabulous Plaza Hotel. But not even the excitement of sharing a rented bed had turned them on. They were husband and wife, no longer a shocking item, and the electricity was gone.

She stopped for a light at Fourteenth Street. What on earth was she doing, reliving scenes from her life with John? You didn't have to be Dr. Freud to spot the pattern. There was no better way to escape from the problems of the present than to mull over the problems of the past.

But escape didn't pay the rent. She stopped at the Idle Hour bookshop on Greenwich Avenue, and bought *The New York Times, The Village Voice, Editor and Publisher, Variety,* and *The Soho News.* If some publication were looking for an entertainment writer, one of those papers would have the word. She added the *New York Post* and the *Daily News* to her pile next to the cash register. It wouldn't hurt to check out the gossip columns. There might be an item on some new magazine starting up. Anyway, she had to keep on top of what was happening in show biz, right? *Right.* That's the attitude, she silently congratulated herself, as she staggered out of the store with her burden of newsprint.

As she passed Ray's Pizza on the corner of Eleventh Street and Sixth Avenue, her stomach reminded her that half a glass of beer had been her entire lunch, and here it was almost six o'clock. The oregano-scented air smelled heavenly, but the line was daunting, and she went on. She exchanged neighborly smiles with the men at Barney's Hardware Store, where she bought her gardening supplies.

"We got in the twenty-pound sacks of potting soil," the owner called out. Maggie looked down at the load of newspapers she was carrying, and they both laughed. "Want someone to carry it up for you?" he asked.

"Thanks, I'll come down for it in the morning. I'm not working tomorrow."

At last she'd be able to spend all the time she wanted in her garden, she thought, urging her mind to travel merry avenues. There were lots of wonderful treats she'd finally be able to indulge in. Reading fat novels. Making herb bread with the thyme and sage she'd grown on her rooftop.

A mewing welcomed her as she let herself into her apartment.

"Hello, O'Malley," she greeted her big tom. She'd named the hairy orange beast for a cartoon cat it distinctly resembled, one of her favorite Walt Disney characters, Abraham de Lacey Giuseppe Casey Thomas O'Malley, the swinging Paris alley cat from *The Aristocats*. "Yes, I *am* home a bit early. Nothing to worry about. Just means you get to eat sooner than usual, and I know you're not going to argue about that." O'Malley urged her toward the kitchen. "What'll it be tonight?" she asked him, going to a cupboard. "Chicken or liver? Chicken? Right-o." She opened a packet of moist cat food—the most expensive brand on the market, but how not give O'Malley the best? "Well, O'Malley," she said, as she ran fresh water into his dish, "I suppose you might as well hear it from me. I rashly quit my job. But not to worry. You'll never have to eat dry cat food. And I'm going to treat myself to a bottle of Perrier. With lime."

She showered and changed into jeans and a big old blue Oxford cloth shirt of her father's, then sat down on the living room couch with her Perrier and her papers.

The help wanted columns yielded nothing. Whom had she been kidding? Jobs like hers on *Limelight* were rare jewels. You didn't find them just lying around, waiting to be picked up.

She took a sip of icy mineral water, opened the *News,* and turned to the columns.

A little shudder of disgust ran through her.

There, on page twenty, was a photograph of George MacDonagh, looking sweaty and happy in the embrace of Genevieve Joyce at the Wild Horse Disco.

Never mind that the flamboyant actress was twice George's age, and married. What was he doing at the Wild Horse, anyway, dancing his brains out and posing like some rock star? Getting in the mood for his next picture, his big rock musical, Maggie thought. She hurled the paper to the floor.

"Forget it," she ordered herself. "If he wants to waste his life, that's his business. He doesn't need you to do social work for him."

Her little lecture did no good. No matter what she told herself to the contrary, she couldn't escape from the feverish thought that George needed her very much. She started pacing up and down the living room in sudden agitation. The article she'd written about George had been intended as a magic mirror in which he could see his true self—the self he'd turned his back on. Why had she thrown it into Ben Harris's wastebasket in that dramatic gesture? She should have tried to sell it to another magazine, not for the money or the glory but so that it could reach its intended audience of one.

She sat down at her typewriter—to no avail. The phrases that had flowed from her fingertips that afternoon at *Limelight* eluded her now. She found herself staring dreamily at the typewriter—and seeing only dark hair that was a little too long and pale blue eyes that knew a little too much.

The jangling of the telephone was a welcome interruption. She eagerly reached for the receiver.

"Maggie?" said a voice she didn't quite dare recognize.

"Yes."

"This is George MacDonagh."

"Yes," she said again. It was all she could say. She reached for her Perrier and gulped down half a glassful.

"I called your office," George went on, "and they said you'd gone home. I have to see you."

Her heart sped so, she could scarcely breathe. "I can't—"

"Before you start telling me you can't, tell me this. Did you mean even half the things you said to me at Sardi's about my work?"

"Look," Maggie stammered, "I suppose you think I—"

Again George interrupted her. "For God's sake, don't tell me what you suppose I think. Just answer me straight out. Were all the digs meant to get me off guard, or did you mean what you said?"

Maggie closed her eyes. "I meant every word." She prepared herself for an onslaught of abuse.

To her amazement, George said, "Good. I thought so. Go look out your window."

Maggie carried the telephone across the room. Finally, she thought inanely, she was getting her money's worth out of her extra-long cord.

"Do you see a blue car double-parked in front of your place?" George asked.

She stared down at a sleek royal blue Fleetwood Cadillac dominating the stretch of Sixth Avenue just opposite the entrance to her building. "Yes," she finally got out. "I see it."

"That's my car, and my driver has instructions to bring you up to the Plaza. Don't worry," he added hastily, in a tone one might use with an anxious child, "I'll meet you downstairs. In the Oak Bar. Will you come?"

A hundred different voices clamored for possession of Maggie's mind. "There's no point," she blurted out. Then, lamely, "I'm wearing jeans."

"Are you? Well, they can always come off, can't they?" the scarperer teased. "Oh, you don't like that,

I know," he added, as her silence made itself heard.
"I'll try to be good. I promise. It's art I want to talk
to you about. Small 'a' art, and capital 'A' Art. If you
really loved *Dublin Dreams*, you can't turn me down.
But maybe I misunderstood you. Maybe it was just
another movie in your life. Maybe—"

It was Maggie's turn to do the interrupting. "I'll
come," she said to George MacDonagh.

chapter 6

"I SEE YOU found a skirt," George commented as Maggie sat down at his table. "Cute. Though I'd like to see you in jeans. And out of jeans. Oh," at a look from Maggie. "I wasn't going to do that, was I?"

"I'd hoped not."

George tried his California stare on her again. She made a little face and gazed out the window at the trees of Central Park across Fifty-ninth Street. She only hoped that the feverishness she felt had no external sign, that the pounding in her eardrums wasn't audible across the table.

"You're such a New Yorker," George said sardonically, brushing dark hair back from his forehead. "Only interested in the higher things."

"Look," Maggie began, "I've got a lot to do—"

"Okay, okay. What are you drinking? Another one of those beer milkshakes?" He was sipping on the inevitable neat Ballymacarbery, and though the glass wasn't Waterford crystal, he looked startlingly like his Times Square poster.

"Nothing, thanks," Maggie answered. "I never ate lunch, actually, and a drink would knock me flat."

"Let me buy you dinner, Emerald Eyes. We can just nip down to the Oyster Bar, or—"

"Please, I'm not hungry. Anyway, I have plans." She didn't add that her plans involved no other person and were eminently changeable. "Let's get on with it. You brought me here to talk about films."

"Right. Got that little notebook with you?" He paused dramatically, then went on, "I've decided to postpone the rock musical. I'm going to do something that's been in the back of my mind for a while. I'm taking off for Ireland on Monday. There's a village on the west coast of County Cork called Castlecove. Probably the most beautiful place on God's earth. I'm going to shoot a film there based on the poem *Lament for Art O'Leary*. That's my capital 'A' Art, you see? The poem's about—"

"I know what it's about," Maggie interrupted. Her heart raced, and not just because of the confoundingly thrilling presence of George MacDonagh. The *Lament for Art O'Leary* was one of her favorite pieces of literature—a haunting epic poem, tender and homey and sensual and political, written by an eighteenth-century woman, Eileen O'Leary, after her young husband was shot by the British. The one movie director capable of bringing its song and its sorrow to the screen was George MacDonagh—the George MacDonagh who had made *Dublin Dreams* while still a student at Trinity College in Ireland. Did he just exist, or was the new, slick MacDonagh the only one in town?

"I suppose you're shooting it with a cast of thousands," she tested him. "In CinemaScope. With Linda Lessing in the lead, and music by Micki Brooks and Her Accoustical Guitar."

"Genevieve Joyce will play Eileen. I'll play Art. And here's the really exciting part." The director leaned across the small table. "I'm going to shoot it on videotape. One cameraman and an assistant. RCA has a beauty of a camera out, the TK-76, and I want to prove it's good for more than TV. We'll use available light—nothing more than a couple of aluminum reflectors. Modern dress. Do our own hair and makeup. A real bare-bones production. Let the poem and the location and the acting carry us."

"Shoot in video for theatrical release?"

"Damn straight. You send that darling little two-inch tape to a transform house, and they can turn it into thirty-five millimeter film, and it's gorgeous. Nobody's really exploited that. The video types are running around making forty-hour tapes of fruit bowls sitting on tables, and the folks in Hollywood can't conceive of a production without gaffers and gofers and two assistant directors and enough equipment to sink the QE Two. I'll have the TK-76, an Ampex 3000 recorder, and that's about it. There are tourists who carry more gadgets just to shoot a bunch of boring slides. Where's your notebook, Emerald Eyes? You remember all those details? RCA TK-76. Ampex—"

"I threw my notebook away," Maggie said. She smiled ruefully. "I threw my job away, actually."

"You did?" George's pale blue eyes widened.

"I did. Tell Harriet Mills it was a nice idea for you to call me, but no cigar. I'm no longer at *Limelight*." She scraped back her chair. "So you don't have to waste your—"

"You are a most infuriating woman," the director

announced. His low, taut voice conveyed more rage
than a shout would have done. "I don't take orders
from publicists, or anyone else. You seem to be convinced that I'm hopelessly corrupt, but I had no ul-
terior motive in calling you. I told you I didn't care
what you wrote about me, and I meant it. But you
happened to have a lot to do with my decision to film
the *Lament* instead of the rock musical, and I just
wanted you to know that. I made the mistake of thinking you'd be excited. Frankly, I'm sorry I bothered."

Maggie gulped. She looked over at the next table,
where two beautiful blondes in big hats were laughing
hysterically about someone named Harry, and beyond
them to a table where a young couple were holding
hands, drinking champagne and gazing at each other
with the unmistakable sweet besottedness of new-
lyweds. She looked back at George MacDonagh's
irate face.

If only the day had gone differently, she lamented
silently. If only she'd managed to make friends, or
at least achieve neutrality, with the director whose
early work she so admired. Then she would have
written a very different sort of piece, and she would
still have her job at *Limelight,* and— And if the day
had gone that way, George MacDonagh would be
planning to make a silly rock musical. Instead, thanks
to her, he was going to make what would probably
be a very beautiful film, and a pioneering one, too.
So her confusion and pain were for the best, right?
Right, she answered herself.

"I am excited," she told him in a small voice. "I
think you've made a wonderful decision. I'm sorry
I'm not going to get to break the story."

"You're an impulsive woman, aren't you? You
certainly looked employed a few hours ago."

"My editor and I had a difference of opinion."

"And you quit? Emerald Eyes, you surely give a

hard time to people who don't see things the way you do. Want to work for me?" He leaned back in his chair and looked at her expectantly.

"I do wish you wouldn't call me Emerald Eyes," she began. Then, "What did you say?"

"Want a job on the *Art O'Leary* production? Or are you going to take advantage of being at-large to go lie on a beach in California?"

"I hate California. I hate beaches. I burn in two minutes." She still couldn't believe he'd said what he'd said.

"Then come to Castlecove," he urged. "Probably no one ever got a sunburn there. I'm traveling light, but I'll still need a unit publicist. Someone to send inspired releases to the American press and stir up interest in what we're doing. And someone to be a liaison with the locals, too. Think you could sell me instead of knocking me? Assuming I stick to the good and true, of course."

"But you don't understand," Maggie blurted out. "I quit my job because my editor thought my piece was too critical of you. I called you a sell-out. How could you want me to work with you?"

"Sure, and it's that nasty way of yours that makes me want to have you hovering about," he rejoined in his hokiest Irish lilt.

Ireland! Art O'Leary! George MacDonagh! A job! Maggie could scarcely believe she'd been offered so many riches all at once.

Except that she couldn't possibly say yes to the offer, she told George.

The dark-haired director sighed into his whiskey. "You break my heart, Emerald Eyes. A fellow you can't leave behind?"

"My private life is none of your business," she shot back. "You may like making love on dance floors while the photographers focus on you, but I don't happen to share that interest. I can't take the job because I can't lie and hype people, and that's what press agents do. Bring Harriet Mills. She can write about you kissing the Blarney Stone."

"Forget Harriet. Harriet and I are through. It's you I need. My red-headed hairshirt."

"I'm glad I amuse you, but—"

"Shhh," he commanded soothingly. For the second time that day, he reached over and probed the tautness of her neck. "So tight I can practically hear it twanging."

"Please," she all but whimpered. "Please don't touch me." She closed her eyes. If he didn't take his hand off her, she was going to rip open the buttons of her own shirt. She was going to crawl under the table and press her lips to his anklebones. Oh, God, the humiliation of feeling what a hundred groupies had felt.

"You need a dose of Ireland, Emerald Eyes," George said, letting his hand fall to the table. "Beats hot tubs. Beats shiatsu massage. The greenest hills, and the sea right there. You'll relax right down to your very soul."

"But I don't want to relax!" Maggie cried out. Her mind suddenly swelled with the memory of the picture she'd seen in the *News* of George MacDonagh and Genevieve Joyce in their glistening disco embrace. "I know the *Lament* will be a very important film, and I'm glad you made the decision you made, and I'm truly pleased if I influenced you, but I can't go to Ireland with you, and that's all there is to it."

"Final decision?" the director asked. His eyebrows danced mockingly. "No appeal?"

Maggie stole another glance at the two honeymooners. They'd looped their arms so they could sip from each other's glasses. The man had a good fifteen years on the woman, and Maggie wondered if their union had shocked the world, as hers and John's had. Would their desire for each other persist even when the shock had worn off, or would it flicker and die like a flame starved of oxygen?

For one brief instant she let her eyes travel the planes of George's face. His features were uncharacteristically still, the eyes neither probing nor darting, the eyebrows at rest, the mouth simply there instead of flashing its usual cocky grin. Even impassive, he had the damnable power to make her feel all but out of control, unacceptably vulnerable. Why wasn't anything ever halfway with her? Why did she always feel one deadly extreme or another? Why was it always fire or ice?

"No appeal," she said.

chapter 7

AND THEN HISTORY HAPPENED.

Maggie Devlin of the singing pride and stinging wit, Maggie Devlin whose high school nickname had been Temper Storm, Maggie Devlin who had been described as "five foot nine and a half—all of it backbone," *that* Maggie Devlin did something she could not remember having done before.

She changed her mind. She decided to accept George MacDonagh's offer of a job.

Tracy Nichols, her roommate, had something to do with it. She came home from work, heard about the offer George had made, and—showing her own backbone—braved Maggie's wrath and called her twenty-seven kinds of idiot for turning down his offer. Tracy swung high, swung low, and if some of her blows were dirty, so be it. She said she wasn't going to stand by and let her friend throw away the chance of a lifetime.

"You claim you care about art," Tracy exploded, "yet you decide not to work with, to influence, a man whose art you respect like no one else's. Why? Because you think that for a reporter to work as a publicist is to be a turncoat. Bull. There are corrupt reporters, and there are honest publicists. I would have thought you had brains and guts enough to redefine the job. I guess I was wrong."

Tracy glared, took a deep breath, and started again. "You're scared to go to Ireland with George Mac-Donagh because you're attracted to him. Don't try denying it, you've got color in your cheeks I haven't seen for months. It's time you stopped playing the wounded divorcee, scared to love again. You're twenty-four. Are you going to spend the rest of your life going out with the Lou Benjamins of the world— nice, safe guys you don't stand a chance of falling for?"

"I think this is what's known as being read the riot act," Maggie said, a little shakily, as Tracy paused. "Is that all?"

"No, it isn't," said the steamed-up Tracy. "You could try thinking practically for once. It's almost summer, and you know how publishing slows down. You'll get some two-bit job on *Mattress Ticking Manufacturers' Monthly* . . . if you're lucky. And you'll start to hate me, because I'll be making good money and running off to do stories on Yoko Ono."

"I could never hate anyone so honest," Maggie declared, giving her friend an impulsive hug. "And so brave," she added, "considering that I have about six inches on you! And now I'm going off to Ray's to have some pizza and digest all this food for thought you've given me."

Despite two missed meals, Maggie barely managed to eat a slice of pizza. She spent the next half hour walking the crooked streets of Greenwich Village, trying hard not to admit to herself how much truth there had been in Tracy's tirade.

But it was John Venable, Maggie's ex-husband, who was really responsible for her unprecedented change of mind. She returned from her walk to find him sitting on the couch, drinking white wine with Tracy.

John rose as Maggie walked in, and they went through their usual ritual—the brief kiss on the cheek, the exclamations over how good the other looked. In fact, Maggie thought that John looked tired, and she knew she had tomato sauce on her face, but she'd about used up her quota of blunt truth for the day.

"To what do we owe the honor?" Maggie asked with a lightness she didn't feel. John called now and then to impart news he thought would interest her— most recently when his younger sister had given birth to twins. He'd never before just dropped in, and his unexpected presence filled her with anxiety.

"I was down here to talk to someone at N.Y.U.," John said. New York University dominated Washington Square, a few blocks away. "I started walking uptown because it was such a splendid night, and then I realized I was walking by your building. After all," smiling meaningfully, "I've forwarded a lot of mail to this address. Nice little place you've got. Tracy was just about to show me your famous garden."

"I'll let you take over the tour, Maggie," Tracy said, getting to her feet. "I'm going to the Mizzen Head. Come join me if you want." She left, looking a little wistful, Maggie thought. Tracy's divorce had been even more traumatic than her own—her husband had left her for another woman. Nearly every evening she went to the Mizzen Head, a Village bar beloved of writers and political people, many of whom shared Tracy's passion for jogging. Sometimes she didn't come home until the wee hours.

"Well," Maggie said to John. "Let's go upstairs and look at the radishes." She felt faintly uncomfortable sitting alone on the couch with him. There was neither the ease of intimacy nor the protection of formality to define their current connection.

"In a minute. Why don't you get a wine glass? I happened to pick up this Pouilly-Fumé at the little shop across the street—it's quite respectable."

"Knowing I'd have nothing drinkable here," Maggie teased.

"Oh, now, Maggie. You really do look splendid, you know."

Maggie gave him an affectionate little smile. "Every woman should have an ex–husband who tells her she looks splendid when she's got Ray's pizza all over her face. Do you still hate pizza?"

"I'm allergic to tomatoes, remember?"

"Oh, that's right." Astonishing what a person could forget about another person. John had always been a great one for allergies. At first Maggie had found the allergies strangely endearing—welcome imperfections in the Great Man. Then, when they were married and living together, the dozens of sensitivities to everything from no-iron sheets to walnuts had become a source of irritation for her.

Well, John's allergies were his problem alone now, she told herself. Or were they someone else's problem, too? Her heart fluttering for an instant, she wondered if the reason for his visit was to tell her that there was going to be a new Mrs. John Venable.

John took her hand, and Maggie braced herself for the announcement. She all but fell over when John said instead, "Maggie, I've missed you unbearably much. I've gone out with a dozen women since you, and no one has come close to taking your place in my heart, in my arms. I think we gave up too soon. We never even got around to talking about children. We—"

"John. John," Maggie stopped him gently. Looking at him, she saw the same man who'd so impressed her one fall day when he'd come striding into a classroom to conduct a seminar on modern European theater. The thick, wavy hair was still the color of oatmeal. The brown eyes were still keen and compelling behind the horn-rimmed glasses. The six-foot frame, pounded to leanness on the squash courts of academe, still had an aristocratic grace in the regulation Ivy League khaki suit he wore. At forty-two, John Venable didn't have to be lonely.

But recognizing that a man was attractive was one thing, and being attracted to him was another. John Venable was no longer the Olympian professor playing to Maggie's impressionable student. Searching her innermost self, she could find only a friendly fondness for him, coupled with a wistful regret that their passion for each other had been a brush fire, quickly extinguished, not the eternal flame they'd mistaken it for.

"John," she said now, "you were forever talking in the classroom about history repeating itself. And I know that's what would happen with us. We might manage to have one fine fling, just because it's so exotic to go out with the person you've divorced, but once dear old everyday reality set in..." Her voice trailed off and she shook her head. "We'd pretty quickly rediscover that we're two very different people."

"You're tired," was all John said. "Tracy told me about your quitting your job. I guess you've had all you could handle today. I should have waited for a riper moment to approach you, but when I saw you, I had to say what's been on my mind for weeks." He took off his glasses and mopped his forehead with a tattersall handkerchief. Maggie remembered giving him the handkerchief in the days when she was trying to be a perfect wife, and her emotions churned.

John stood up. "I'll let you go to bed, young woman. But I'm not giving up. They're reviving *Happy End* at the Yale Repertory. Maybe I can persuade you to drive to New Haven with me. We'll stop somewhere along the shore for lobster. I— Good heavens, Maggie, you could have warned me," as Abraham de Lacey Giuseppe Casey Thomas O'Malley came bounding into the room. John ostentatiously blew his nose into the tattersall handkerchief. "You know I'm allergic to cats. Can't you—"

"Scoot, O'Malley," Maggie ordered, giving the orange beast a gentle swat on his behind. He took the hint and scampered back toward Maggie's bedroom. She promised herself to reward him later with extra milk. Milk, hell. She'd give him cream.

John held out his arms and said, "I'll call you on Monday. You'll be yourself on Monday."

Maggie leaned against his chest, hearing the thuds of his heart, then eased herself out of his embrace. "Didn't Tracy tell you about the fantastic job I've been offered?" she asked, over the sudden thuds of her own heart. "I won't be here on Monday. I'm going to work for George MacDonagh. I'm going to Ireland."

chapter 8

"NOT HUNGRY, NOW? Is that a fact? Sure you'd not say no to a sliver of smoked salmon. Goes down like silk, it does. I'll leave you a wee portion, so."

The rosy cheeked, raven-haired Aer Lingus stewardess smiled at Maggie Devlin and set a plate of thinly sliced smoked salmon in front of her. Maggie managed to produce a smile in return. She was certainly suffering in style, she had to admit. She'd never flown first class before, and she was frankly dazzled by the opulent service aboard the green and white 747. The smoked salmon was carved to order and served on delicate Tara china; her Harp-on-the-rocks had been presented in a diamond-cut Waterford crystal goblet with a faceted stem. There was a luxurious sense of space. For once the long-legged Maggie didn't feel that an aircraft had been designed with some other species of passenger in mind. The twenty-four privileged people in the curtained-off cabin sat two by comfortable two. Up an inviting swirl of steps there was a private bar, with room to do everything but disco. And a bevy of what her seatmate called hot and cold running cabin attendants was doing everything possible to see that all wants were satisfied.

Suffering in style; suffering nonetheless. Better to be on the hottest, most crowded, ricketiest old bus somewhere and have the world under control, have herself under control, than to be feeling the agony she felt right now. Damn and double damn George MacDonagh. Damn herself for a fool.

Her stomach knotted as she peered over the intervening rows and looked at the back of George's head. His dark hair hung down over the collar of his sixty-dollar designer workshirt. Genevieve Joyce's famous mane of dark curls mingled with the director's hair as she cozied up to his shoulder.

You knew what he was all about from the beginning, Maggie reminded herself sternly, forcing her eyes to turn away from the cruel yet somehow thrilling sight of the dark hair. She looked out her small, cold window at the streaks of sunset across the night sky, apricots and purples, but her eyes had a mind of their own, a strange kind of lust for torment, and they strayed back toward the first row of the cabin.

"Stay cool," Tracy Nichols had advised her, as Maggie was packing her suitcases in their Greenwich Village apartment—trying to decide if she could live without her pale blue shetland sweater, and if one swimsuit would do. "Keep the lid on your temper, and you'll get everything you want. No, don't take that sweater. You'll want to buy sweaters in Ireland."

The trouble, Maggie thought now, twenty-six thousand feet above sea level and climbing, was that she didn't know what she wanted—sweaters aside.

The past few days had been too chaotic for anything like clear thinking; raw nerve endings were the order of the hour. George had flown back to California the morning after Maggie had phoned him to say she would, after all, like to be the unit publicist for the *Lament for Art O'Leary*. She'd been left to define her new job and get down to it, as well as shop for the trip, make financial arrangements with Tracy, talk for hours on the telephone with her parents, mulch the garden, read up on Ireland, and sneak extra cream to her cat so he wouldn't forget her while she was away.

Three or four coast-to-coast conversations a day with George had only heightened her confusion. On one call he would be pure business; the next, he would make it sound as though the main purpose of the *Art O'Leary* production was to provide Maggie and George with the opportunity to look at the moon over Castlecove harbor.

"Of course he wants you. Of course you want him," Tracy Nichols had announced more than once. But that was Tracy's version of life. All attractive people wanted one another, and had one another, unless they were hung-up on some weary so-called moral code. Once, after a phone call during which George had made a point of saying it was so beastly hot that he had taken off his clothes and was walking around "starkers," Maggie had desperately wished she were more like Tracy. She would give in to the pulsing heat provoked by George MacDonagh. She would foreswear all claims to dignity and join his infernally long list of bed partners. At least there would be the satisfaction of feeling her flesh sing again, the reassurance that divorce hadn't maimed her for life, and the knowledge that she was still a whole woman.

But was the choice hers? She wasn't sure it was, now, and that was the most bitter ingredient in the stew of her confusion. There was George in the first row of the cabin with Genevieve Joyce, seemingly unaware that there was anyone else in the aircraft. And here was Maggie, back in the smoking section, with one Lorenzo F. X. Delgado. She supposed it was only proper, the director sitting with the star, and the press agent sitting with the newsman. But what about the phone call during which George had talked about the flight to Ireland as their private magic-carpet ride? Oh, the shamelessness of the man!

"Don't you ever relax, Devlin?"

"What?" she asked Larry Delgado.

"Don't you ever relax? Look at your fists, Devlin. So tight your knuckles are white. Fear of flying?"

"No, and I wish people would stop asking me to relax. Relaxation is one of the overrated pleasures of the twentieth century. Creeping California-ism, that's what it is. No one ever accomplished anything by being laid-back."

"Excuse me, Devlin. I didn't realize you were 'accomplishing' at the moment." He raised his scotch and water to her.

He seemed more amused than irritated by her shortness, but she knew she'd been rude, and she was angry with herself. The rumpled, balding newsman was only aboard Aer Lingus flight 104 to Shannon because she'd called him at his Chicago office and invited him to join the MacDonagh party in Castlecove and file a series of columns on the making of *Lament for Art O'Leary*. That he'd accepted was really quite a coup for a fledgling publicist. Lorenzo F. X. Delgado was maybe the most powerful nationally syndicated movie reviewer in the United States. Four stars from Delgado meant as much at the box office as an Oscar. One star, or—heaven forbid—no stars from Delgado, and producers just curled up and cried. Maggie nearly always admired his reviews. She'd

teasingly suggested to George that they invite Larry
to join them as his reward for having had the good
taste to call *On the Make* "the worst movie ever made
by a truly great director." Now here they all were.

Larry Delgado signaled a stewardess and asked for
another drink. He looked at Maggie's scarcely touched
goblet of Harp.

"You drink beer on the rocks because you really
like it, or because you think it makes you interesting?"
He proffered a pack of unfiltered cigarettes, smiled
at Maggie's vehement head shake, then lit up for
himself. He took a great draught of his fresh drink,
as if it, too, were beer.

"I didn't know it made me interesting," Maggie
replied, trying not to sound as ill-tempered as she felt.

"Devlin, you are very interesting," Larry Delgado
said, with the air of a man uttering large truths. "It
may be the beer, or the ink smudge on your right
wrist, or it may be the way you smell. I'll let you
know which," he added solemnly. "Do you wash your
hair with apple juice?"

Maggie's heart sank. She hoped fervently that
Larry wasn't going to turn out to be one of those
decent men who underwent a personality change when
they'd had too much to drink. He'd been going at it
pretty steadily, starting back at the Aer Lingus V.I.P.
lounge, the Tara Club, at Kennedy Airport. Thanks
to George MacDonagh, she was stuck with the man
for the next five hours or so. She stole a look at him.
His balding head was glistening with sweat. His neck
was disconcertingly red.

"Does your wife wash her hair with apple juice?"
she asked, with what she hoped was a killing inno-
cence.

"Devlin," he came back, "if my wife's hair smelled
as good as yours, you think I would have left her for
four weeks? Only kidding," he added, as Maggie

made evident her distaste at the remark. "Great gal, my wife. Best friend I have in the world. But there is there and here is here, as Mr. Cole Porter never wrote. You're probably too young to know who Cole Porter is. Smartest songwriter who ever lived. I suppose you listen to music by people with names like Hot Tuna." He shook his head. "Hot Tuna."

"I love Cole Porter," Maggie enthused, happy to be on more neutral ground. "'At Long Last Love' was the theme song at my wedding." Her smile growing wistful, she added, "I guess 'Just One of Those Things' would have been more appropriate."

"You've been through the wars, too, eh?" Larry consolingly patted her hand, let his touch linger an instant too long, then withdrew his own hand just as Maggie was about to protest. "Divorced?" Larry asked.

"Yes," Maggie said, regretting that she'd let the talk turn personal again. She didn't relish the idea of swapping life stories with Larry Delgado. "Seen any good movies lately?" she asked brightly.

"Okay, I can take a hint," he returned good-naturedly. To Maggie's great relief, he took the Aer Lingus magazine out of the seat pocket in front of him and began doing the crossword puzzle. Finishing the puzzle, he drained his scotch and water and softly whistled another Cole Porter melody, 'Let's Fly Away.' Maggie closed her eyes and leaned back to enjoy his surprising tunefulness. Suddenly she felt his touch again, this time on her thigh. Her eyes flew open.

"Larry—" she began sternly.

"Did I do that?" he asked, blinking, looking at the trespassing fingers of his right hand as if they were foreign objects. His left hand reached over to bring the straying right hand back to home territory. He

grinned—a sheepish grin that made it hard for Maggie
to be really angry at him. "Nobody gets near you
except El Genius, is that it?" he asked.

A suddenly thick-tongued Maggie stammered, "I
don't know what you mean."

"Aw, don't play the innocent with me, will you,
Devlin? I've seen you look at MacDonagh. I've seen
him look at you, as far as that goes."

"You're quite mistaken," Maggie said, as coolly
as she could. "I'm here because I admire him as a
filmmaker. And his interests are all too apparent."

Larry followed her bitter glance the length of the
cabin. George and Genevieve appeared to be laughing
together—sharing some intimate joke, Maggie imagined. All at once they stood up. For one heart-stopping
moment Maggie imagined they were on their way to
the upstairs bar, and would have to pass the row where
she sat with Larry, but instead they turned the other
way. To Maggie's shock and horror, they vanished
together into the lavatory at the front of the cabin.

"Maybe they want to rehearse in private?" Larry
suggested.

His clumsy attempt at consoling Maggie only deep-
ened her feeling of humiliation. Mumbling that she
desperately needed to stretch her legs, she eased past
Larry and fled up the curving steps to the first class
lounge. She ordered a Perrier and struck up a conversation with Adam Manski, the Polish émigré cinematographer whom George had coaxed into joining
the production company. Adam's grasp of English
was impressive, and his store of technical knowledge
even more so, and in no time at all he had Maggie
deep in a discussion about cameras and lighting.

"You mean we won't be able to shoot at midday?"
she asked, after he made some points about the pitfalls
of shooting with natural light.

"That's right," a deep voice answered from behind her. "You wouldn't want to see shadows under Genevieve's eyebrows, would you?"

Holding onto her icy glass of mineral water to keep her body temperature from escalating, Maggie slowly turned to look at George MacDonagh.

"Where *is* Genevieve?" she couldn't help asking. "I thought you two went everywhere together."

If George heard the barb in the question, he ignored it. "She's deeply involved with a slice of pâté," he drawled. "All the years we've been friends, and I never knew she was wild about pâté with pistachio nuts in it. There's always another mystery to unravel about people, isn't there, Emerald Eyes?"

"Excuse me, please," Adam interrupted, "but if dinner is served, I must go downstairs." The fair-haired, slightly built man patted a concave stomach. "I have not eaten since California."

"You keep up your strength," George ordered affectionately. "Ask the stewardess to give you my pâté, too. I'd just as soon eat liverwurst. Actually," he added, as Adam moved out of earshot, "I'd just as soon nibble on you." He dropped into the seat Adam had left vacant. His pale blue eyes played over Maggie's face. He planted an impish kiss on her nose. "Having fun? I love flying. Actually, we ought to be back in tourist class. Any minute someone's bound to whip out an accordian, and everyone will start singing 'The Rose of Tralee,' 'Danny Boy'...don't you love it?"

Maggie shrugged, and said stiffly, "My Uncle Pat used to sing all that stuff."

"You mentioned him on the phone. I think I'd like this Uncle Pat of yours. You know, Emerald Eyes, you were the one who all but pushed me to go back to Ireland and make another film there. But half the time you almost seem to want to deny that you're

Irish. A little conflict in the complicated soul of Maggie Devlin?"

"Maybe," was all Maggie could say. She was having a hard time believing that George could sit entwined with Genevieve Joyce, actually disappear into the lavatory with her, and then beam so much coziness Maggie's way. Was there no limit to the man's appetite? Or was he playing some kind of game, trying to sew up the devotion of his publicist so she'd work all the harder for him? The engines changed pitch, and she thought she would sooner understand the intricacies of a 747 than the workings of George MacDonagh. With him, there wouldn't always be one more mystery to unravel; there would always be a thousand more.

Now he gave her his California guru gaze, his eyes forcing hers to meet his in one of those awful contests to see who could force the other's gaze to waver first. "Are you mad at me?" George asked, with a directness that matched the stare.

Averting her eyes and conceding the match, Maggie said, "No. Not exactly."

"Are you glad at me?"

"Sad at you," she answered, with a half-smile.

"Why?" George persisted.

She wanted to run away from his questions, or deflect them with clever quips, yet a part of her heaved a sigh of relief at being forced into simple honesty. "Because we're so different," she said.

George reached over and ran a finger across the apple of her cheek—a tiny caress which made Maggie feel as though the jet had hit an air pocket and fallen a thousand feet.

"Is it so awful when I touch you, Emerald Eyes?" he asked, as she folded her arms across her chest to ward off what felt like a threat by her body to explode with ecstasy.

Unable to speak, she just shook her head.

"I know you're only interested in me professionally," George began. "But I have a right to try to change your mind, don't I?"

Again, Maggie thought of Genevieve—and of the countless other women who had been linked with George. "What's the use?" she blurted out unhappily. "I told you, we're just too different. I can't care about more than one person at a time. It's all or nothing for me."

"But—"

Maggie put gentle fingers to George's lips, sealing them shut. "I've heard all the arguments. Let me just be your press agent. I better go back to Larry."

George raised his thick eyebrows, and abruptly pushed back the dark shock of hair on his forehead. For an instant Maggie would have sworn that the light was gone from his eyes, and they'd paled to the color of ice, but then he grew animated again. "No sacrifice too great, as long as it's in the name of art?" he queried sardonically. "Do go back to Larry. And do keep him very happy."

Maggie felt herself flush with anger. "What exactly are you suggesting?"

"I believe you're the one who did the suggesting," George said coldly.

For a moment, Maggie simply looked at George. Then she shook her head and turned away. What was the point in further discussion? Clearly she and George were doomed to irritate each other. She'd always suspected that California was spiritually further away from New York than any other place on earth, and now she knew she'd been right. Much as she ordinarily loved being right, she wished that, just this once, she'd been wrong.

chapter 9

MAGGIE OPENED HER EYES, looked out the car window, then closed her eyes again. She had to be dreaming. Or maybe she'd died and gone to Oz? In the real world, the landscape wasn't so singingly green, and the green didn't come in so many shades and tones, a kind of spectrum unto itself—shimmering, tranquil, blindingly beautiful.

She let the hum of the car lull her back into the twilight zone halfway between sleeping and waking. So pleasant just to go with the motion of the low-slung Mercedes, and smell the leather of the upholstery, and feel the dear broad bones of George MacDonagh's shoulder beneath her head—

What? Her head jerked up. How on earth—?

"Is Sleeping Beauty stirring?" she heard Genevieve

Joyce inquire sardonically from the other side of George.

"Shhh," George answered softly, as Maggie moaned restlessly, the way a dreamer would, and settled back against him for one moment of peace wrested out of chaos. She wasn't really faking, she told herself guiltily, trying to catch hold of the tail end of a dream and ride it back into unconsciousness. It wasn't as if she *wanted* to be awake. She felt her breathing flatten out as the morning reconstructed itself in a series of pleasant still shots...

Larry Delgado having one sip of scotch too many aboard the flight to Shannon, falling asleep, and leaving Maggie in something like contentment, free to delve into her copy of the *Art O'Leary* script as she nibbled on quail's eggs, rare filet mignon, rich Galtee cheese, and wonderfully grainy bread with sweet Kerrygold butter. The 747 landing at Shannon just after seven in the morning in a misty sky that boasted a rainbow. Adam Manski, George's cameraman, loading the exalted TK-76, Ampex recorder, and portable aluminum light reflectors into a rented van. Larry— sober and restored to civility—offering to keep him company on the four-hour drive to Castlecove. A heavyset but handsome, soft-spoken man in his seventies named Tom Farley ushering Maggie, George, and Genevieve Joyce into the back of his gray Mercedes.

As they'd driven away from Shannon, her first few glimpses of Ireland had been as perfect as postcards. She'd seen double-decker buses painted a merry red and children with cheeks nearly as red, sheep grazing peacefully on the grassy slopes to either side of the road, and a turreted castle older than any other building she'd ever seen. Listening to George produce humorous limericks as they passed through the outskirts of Limerick, Maggie had found herself thinking that

Ireland was magical, and too beautiful a place to spoil with harsh judgments of other people. Maybe there was even magic enough to build a rainbow bridge between a New Yorker and Californian, she'd thought dreamily, as she'd collapsed into sleep.

Now through the filters of her twilight zone Maggie heard Genevieve whisper to George, "Darling, I'm not sure I can wait much longer."

"We should be there in less than hour," George answered. "Forty-five minutes, really. Think you can hang on? It'd be much more comfortable at the inn."

"Oh, no," Maggie groaned inwardly, feeling her new ease and benevolence evaporating like a dream shattered by the ringing of an alarm clock. She thought about coughing to announce her wakefulness, but the muscles in her throat felt paralyzed. She willed her ears to seal themselves off; she begged sleep to reclaim her. All to no avail.

George leaned forward to ask Tom Farley if there were a good spot to have lunch between there and Castlecove, and Tom Farley said Kathleen and Bryan would be disappointed not to be giving them their first meal on Irish soil. There *was* a pub in Bandon that did a grand lunch, though, toasted sandwiches and an apple tart with cream. For one brief moment Maggie happily called herself a fool—it had been food that Genevieve couldn't wait for.

Then Genevieve said: "Can we have Tom drop Little Miss Maggie off at this pub and take a spin around the block before we go in ourselves? I'm getting a bit tired of doing it in the loo."

"You know, gorgeous, you're going to have to learn to do it in public," Maggie's incredulous ears heard George say under his breath. Maggie's mind reeled. George wasn't planning to make an X-rated *Art O'Leary,* was he? The script she'd read on the plane had the muted sensuality of the poem it was based on. But the director was famous for departing from his scripts once the shooting started.

"I know," Genevieve sighed. "So tiresome, darling. My dear old hubby would be devastated if he knew I was being this back street about it. That's the trouble with being married to a doctor. They're so matter-of-fact about the body."

"He's right, you know," George said. Maggie thought she heard the sentence being punctuated by the placing of denim arms around rustling silk shoulders.

"That's easy for you to say. It isn't your body that's taking all the abuse." Genevieve's voice had a dramatic little catch to it. "My thighs are black and blue. It's a good thing I won't have any bikini scenes. Are you sure that Superflack is still asleep, by the way? I don't want this getting in the papers. She might just think that my little secret would make great copy."

"Come, come. I didn't bring Maggie to Ireland to make my star miserable." Denim stroked silk again.

"Why did you bring the dear thing? If I couldn't bring Penzi to do my hair because we're being so 'bare bones,' I hardly see why we need a unit publicist," Genevieve sulked. "An amateur at that."

"Listen, pet, Maggie handed me my head during that interview at Sardi's. Interview, hell. Inquisition was what it was. I wanted to pay her back."

"You sly devil," Genevieve applauded throatily.

Maggie ground her teeth together. Her stomach did flip flops. Why, oh why, hadn't she announced her wakefulness while she could do so with grace? She was being well and truly punished for the sin of eavesdropping, that was for sure. If there had been a more wretched moment in her life, she couldn't recall it. She wished Tom Farley would drive into a ditch. She wished the world would simply end.

A blessed silence followed. Well, almost blessed.

Her mind kept spinning on what she'd just heard. The invitation to join the *Art O'Leary* company had been nothing but a set-up. The chauffeur-driven car outside her Village apartment, the flattering words about her influence, the honeyed phone calls about the moon over Castlecove harbor—all had been part of the same diabolical game.

How could she have been so thick, so gullible, so vain as to think that George MacDonagh really valued her professionally, longed for her personally? Sure, he'd be happy if he got some work out of her, but to a man of his means the cost of an air ticket and her salary was a small price to pay to see her squirm. She just wished that Ben Harris at *Limelight* could have some idea of how the man operated, of how more than justified she'd been in saying that George MacDonagh's love affair with himself was one of the great romances of the century. A man who could call on his tremendous powers of creativity to devise such elaborate retribution for a few well-intentioned hard questions—that was one of the oversized egos not just of the century but of all time.

Well, George MacDonagh was in for a surprise. George MacDonagh was going to find out that his nasty little plan was less than the marvel he imagined it to be. Let him do his worst. Let him make her want to die a thousand deaths. He would see nothing but smiles. You can't humiliate someone who refuses to be humiliated, right? *Right*, she silently answered herself.

She felt the car slow down. At last this phase of her torment would end.

"Here we be," Tom Farley called from the front seat.

A hand gently shook Maggie's shoulder. George's hand. She noted with self-congratulation that her flesh reacted with icy calm to the touch the mere thought of which had not long ago ignited wild fantasies.

"What?" she exclaimed, with what she hoped was convincing sleep-befuddlement. She sat up. She yawned. She blinked. She stretched. "Where are we? Have I been asleep long?"

George puckered his lips as if to whistle—the signal, Maggie now recognized, that a limerick was forthcoming.

"A young reporter who came from New York
"To make Art in the County of Cork
"Spent her first hours in Eire
"Authoring snores, I fear,
"Oh, that noisy young nose from New York."

"Darlings, did I snore?" she cried gaily, smothering her impulse to slug. "How too awfully boring of me!" Genevieve's famous huge brown velvet eyes rolled her way, and Maggie looked out the car window to hide her grin of satisfaction. "Is this Castlecove?"

"Bandon. It's another forty-five minutes or so to the inn," George said, "and Tom suggested the Glasslyne Pub as a good place for lunch."

"Pub grub! I love it," exclaimed the reborn Maggie.

As Tom guided the big car down the narrow main street, Maggie reveled in what she saw. The shops were all joined at the seams, or separated by the narrowest of alleys, but each façade was painted a different color, each more edible than the next—a lime-green butcher shop, a lemon sherbet tobacconist's, a honey vanilla fishmonger's, a strawberry frappé clothing shop. The jumbled colors broke up space and gave the effect of an enchanting mosaic.

Maggie watched the women of the town, most of them with several small children in their wake, wander in and out of the shops. For a moment she pictured herself going about the life here rather than in the considerably more frantic city of New York. But there was no time for reverie. She scanned windows and signs, looking for a plausible reason to say she wanted to get out of the car and meet the others at the Glasslyne Pub, thereby depriving George and Genevieve of the satisfaction of dumping her before they had their squalid little feel-on-wheels.

"Good heavens," she suddenly exclaimed. "Look, over there. G. P. Devlin, Chemist. Chemist means pharmacy, doesn't it? My father is G. P. Devlin. Gerald Patrick Devlin. I suppose it's only coincidence, but would you mind if I ran in for a minute? Maybe they're long-lost cousins. At least I can probably buy my father some soap with their name on it. I'll meet you at the pub. I see it ahead there on the left. That'll give you time to—"

She broke off in a panic. Had she gone too far? Given her eavesdropping away?

"—to find a parking place," she tried, wondering if her voice were squeaking in reality or only in her imagination. "Though people seem to park anywhere here," she added recklessly, only to wonder if Tom Farley would feel she'd insulted the Irish. "Of course they do in New York, too. Remember what a disaster it was when the mayor put bike lanes on the major avenues? Triple parking at rush hour." On that note, feeling a total idiot, hoping desperately that her blathering would be ascribed to jet lag, she hopped out of the gray Mercedes and ran across the street.

chapter 10

"OH!" MAGGIE EXCLAIMED genuinely, as Tom Farley's Mercedes started down a curving sweep of road, and Castlecove harbor was revealed in all its glory. "Oh!" she cried again. The beauty of the place was too staggering for any reaction but that eternal expression of awe. Mr. G. P. Devlin, the Bandon chemist, had said he had no kin the United States, but who needed Mr. G. P. Devlin of Bandon? Maggie's blood sang as she stared out the window. The landscape moved her as no other ever had. She had come home at last.

The sight of sea and hill together was, for Maggie, always thrilling. Here the beauty was compounded by the absolute blue of the water and those endlessly varied greens, patchworked out to the horizon, of the surrounding hills. A spit of land tricked the eye into seeing the hills as a linked entity, cupping the harbor. So for all the grandeur of the scene below, it was finite and accessible—a natural spectacle enhanced, not marred, by such signs of civilization as the sailboats in the harbor and the houses along the road.

George leaned over Maggie's shoulder to share the view from the window. He seemed as excited as a small boy.

"Not bad, is it?" Tom Farley said, with unmistakable pride. "Change a lot since you last saw it, George?"

George burst out laughing at the tease. Castlecove harbor had changed less in the last ten years, he said, than Los Angeles had changed in the last ten minutes.

"You'll not find the inn changed much either, though there's a grand new bath in the room you'll be having, Miss Joyce, and my Kathleen's done wonders with the garden."

"You know, Tom, it's going to be a bit of a shock to me, seeing Kathleen all grown-up. And what about this husband of hers?"

"Bryan Dunstable's a fine lad."

"I don't doubt it," George bantered, "but I thought Kathleen was going to wait for me."

"It's a good thing she didn't," Tom said tartly. "You took your time getting back, did you not. Well, maybe you'll find yourself an Irish wife, now you're here. It's time you were settling down, George. Kathleen and Bryan, they've four children, and the only sorrow is that my Máire didn't live to see them. Shelagh, that's the four year old, looks so like Máire as nearly breaks my heart.

George leaned forward and briefly clasped the driver's shoulder. "I'll miss her, too. I know Máire's presence is everywhere at the inn." Then, after a minute's silence, "You ever see any of my films, Tom?"

"I saw that *Dublin Dreams* you made just after you were here. It was—" He broke off and cleared his throat. "Then there was one came to Skibbereen a year or so ago, and I meant to see it, but—" His voice trailed off, then picked up again. "I've seen all your films, Miss Joyce," he said respectfully, making it a two-syllable word, "fil-ims", and sitting up perceptibly straighter. "I think you're a grand actress, and it's an honor to have you in Castlecove."

"I'm thrilled to be here," Genevieve drawled, so nakedly sarcastic that Maggie could cheerfully have bitten her. But if Tom was wounded, he gave no sign, and Maggie vowed to take a lesson from his impassiveness. That was the way to handle people like Genevieve Joyce and George MacDonagh, all right.

George pointed to a profusion of fuchsia growing alongside the road. "Look at the color. I've got to get that on film. Everyone talks about the greens of Ireland, but I think it's the fuchsia that's stayed in my mind's eye all these years."

"The two together," Maggie said. "The green lulls your eye, and then the red is so sudden."

"Exactly," George exclaimed. "That's how I'll shoot it. A slow pan over those greens, then boom. The red will be like an assault on the senses."

"Am I getting second billing to the shrubbery, darling?" Genevieve asked drily.

Maggie tuned her out. For a moment she forgot everything except the genius of George MacDonagh. Never mind his gargantuan ego. Never mind his sick, elaborate plan for revenge. Never mind his womanizing. He was *the* moviemaker of her generation, and she was working with him, and *Lament for Art O'Leary* would be different for her presence. If only their connection could stay on that professional level. Then she could enjoy her brief season in this gorgeous place.

As the afternoon wore on, her hopes intensified. Castlecove Inn, a great ramble of a white wooden house, instantly felt like home. By five o'clock, as she sat on a wooden stool at the bar of the pub attached to the inn, watching the petite, dark-haired Kathleen Dunstable scrape the cream off the top of a pint of Guinness, then draw more stout from the tap, let the cream rise in the mug, and scrape it off again, Maggie felt with happy irrationality that the universe had conspired to bring her to Castlecove.

"I'll never drink beer on the rocks again," she sighed. She took small sips of the dense, nutty-tasting brew. "So delicious." She looked up at a poster proclaiming, in brown and gold letters: GUINNESS IS GOOD. "For once, truth in advertising."

"The adverts used to say 'Guinness is good for you,' only the government put a stop to that," Kathleen said. "I daresay it's put away a few men before their time," she added cheerfully, "but it's grand for a nursing mother, everyone knows that. Full of minerals. I'd have had a time of it when the twins came without the odd Guinness. It was only—" She stopped herself mid-sentence. She gave a deprecating little shake of her head. "Cow talk," she smiled. "That's what Bryan would call it. With the glamorous life you lead, you don't want to be hearing a lot of chat about mother's milk. Tell me now, Maggie," leaning across the oak bar, "did you ever meet Dustin Hoffman? There's my idea of a bit of heaven. I do think Bryan looks awfully like him, don't you?"

"He does. Absolutely," Maggie answered, hoping she sounded convincing. "The boyish grin, and they're built the same."

"Just so," Kathleen agreed happily. "You've met him, then? Dustin, I mean?"

"A couple of times," Maggie said. "He's nice."

"Nice!" Kathleen echoed, clutching her heart in

mock agony. "All you can say is *nice?* Of course he's not your type, is he? You'd go for the tall ones." She gave a knowing little nod, making Maggie feel all but transparent. Was there anyone who didn't guess, after five minutes with her, that George MacDonagh had a stranglehold on her emotions? "Speaking of the devil," Kathleen added pertly, "here he is. Hello, George."

"Hello, my pretty. Well, well, Ms. Maggie. Not felled by the rigors of travel like the rest of our gang?" Leaving a fleeting fingerprint on Maggie's shoulder, George bellied up to the bar and propped a foot on the lower rung of Maggie's stool. "Genevieve has one of her 'heads,' and when I knocked on Adam's door, he told me to come back next year. Larry said he *may* make it down to dinner."

"I meant to have a nap," Maggie said, "but I had a bath and unpacked and then suddenly I was too excited about being in Ireland to sleep."

She noted with satisfaction that the anesthetic she'd mentally administered to herself earlier in the day was still doing its work. She had absolutely no trouble breathing in George's presence. There were no wild fluctuations in body temperature. She felt neither bruised nor burned where he had touched her. The very slight lightheadedness she was experiencing was entirely attributable to the Guinness she'd consumed—no doubt about it.

She even kept her composure when Kathleen said to George, as if he and Maggie were clearly a couple, "The things your Maggie's done, and only twenty-four."

"I was thinking a minute ago that I couldn't believe you have four kids at twenty-four," Maggie said hastily. "And to run the inn besides. I barely manage to run my share of a three-room apartment. About the only thing I've ever been successfully in charge of is the world's smallest garden, and I may lose it to the birds before the summer's over. I'd love to see your garden. Your father said you've pulled off wonders with it."

"I haven't done so badly," Kathleen conceded, "considering that the soil here isn't rich."

The street door opened at the far end of the pub, and a compact, ruddy-faced man of about sixty, wearing a cloth cap and battered but handsome tweeds, made his way slowly across the floor. Maggie would have sworn that George suddenly tensed. Kathleen, reaching for a glass mug on a shelf behind her, seemed to lose some of her vivacity.

"Here's Liam Keaveny for his pint. You can set your clock by him," Kathleen said to Maggie with a brightness that struck her as forced. "He's had his Harp and his packet of crisps—potato chips to you— every day at this hour for as long as I can remember, and then another round at six, and that's dinner, so. How do you like that for a bit of local color? Evening, Liam."

"Evening, Kathleen." Staring at Maggie and George but not otherwise acknowledging their existence, Liam Keaveny sat down at the opposite end of the bar. "Fine weather we've got today," he said to Kathleen.

"I wouldn't mind a drop of rain for the garden."

Maggie watched admiringly as Kathleen went about her work, an efficient little dynamo in jeans and a fisherman's denim smock. The two of them were going to be fast friends, for sure.

Was it her Irish blood, Maggie wondered, that made her feel so absolutely at home as she sat sipping Guinness at the Castlecove Inn? There was something strangely familiar about the dark wood and low light, the plain tables set against a far wall, and the particular configuration of bottles behind the bar.

Despite her self-inflicted numbness, there was no denying that George MacDonagh was part of the beauty of the scene, too. His long, lean body might have been constructed for standing at this bar. His profile bore a wonderful kinship to the still-handsome face of Liam Keaveny, bent silently over his pint of Harp. The cowboy boots and Levis and green and white striped rugby shirt were the clothes not of a tourist but of a man on home turf.

George broke the uncomfortable silence that had settled over the pub since Liam Keaveny's entrance. "So where's the Ballymacarbery poster with my mug on it?" he teased Kathleen. "I'd have thought you'd have it plastered all over the place . . . loyalty to old friends, and such."

Tossing her shaggy dark hair, Kathleen shot back, "Your image may sell whiskey in the States, but hereabouts, my lad, it isn't worth cuckoo-spit."

"The truth of it is, Kathleen, you've been so busy breeding babies you haven't had time to keep after this place. That Guinness poster is older than Denny, and there's a cobweb up on the ceiling I remember from my last visit."

"The only cobwebs around here are in your brain, George MacDonagh." Kathleen retorted.

Maggie listened enviously, thinking that she was going to have to brush up on her put-downs if she wanted to have an easy time of it with George. Not that a bantering friendship was what she really craved—but then again, she sternly reminded herself, her cravings had officially been put on ice. If only he weren't so damned attractive, and so much a part of the charm of Ireland, almost as if he were a bonus in a package tour, a little something extra designed to enchant even the wariest traveler.

Bringing Maggie welcome relief from her confused thoughts, four-year-old Shelagh Dunstable burst through the swinging doors linking pub and inn, with Tom Farley puffing behind. "Mama, Grandpop has to go into Skib because Miss Joyce has a headache and he says I may go with him if you say I may, and Denny says he'll mind the twins because Papa is busy, so may I go, please, may I?"

"Now, what's this?" Kathleen asked, hand on hips, a little smile on her lips, as she gazed fondly at her breathless red-headed daughter.

"Miss Joyce has a bit of a headache," Tom said, "and she can't take aspirin, it upsets her stomach, and I said as I was free I would drive into Skibbereen, and see what the chemist suggests, so. If we leave right now, we'll catch Casey still open."

Kathleen made a face. "That woman. I knew it the moment I set eyes on her."

"My star," George drawled, "doesn't seem to have many fans of her own sex."

"Oh, that's nothing to do with it," Kathleen said crossly. "Pretty nervy of her, if you ask me, sending Dad off to Skib and him just driven to Shannon and back. Did you even have your tea, Dad?"

"I did, I had a gobbling great meal, and I'll thank you, lass, not to carry on so. I'm not yet as old as Atty Hayes's goat."

"But, Dad, you know you haven't been feeling well lately. If you're going to Skib, why don't you call on Doctor Quinn?"

"Furthermore," Tom Farley went on heedlessly, as if Kathleen were the parent and he the child, "it wasn't Miss Joyce as asked me to drive to Skib. I made the offer freely."

"See?" George interjected with a triumphant air that set Maggie's teeth on edge. Genevieve might be a great actress, and his playmate of the hour, but she was hardly a candidate for sainthood. With a suddenly sinking heart she hoped wasn't reflected on her face,

Maggie recalled the conversation she'd inadvertently overheard on the trip down from Shannon—a dialogue she would have given anything to have wiped from memory.

"Please, Mama, please, please, may I go?" Shelagh asked, making Maggie smile in spite of her leaden heart. The four year old was as winning a child as she'd ever met, and their nearly identical hair color made Maggie feel they had a special connection.

"Shelagh Mary," Liam called from the other end of the bar, "would you like a crisp?" He held out the small packet of potato chips. So the mysterious Liam Keaveny wasn't all rudeness and gloom, Maggie thought.

"Oh, yes, please," Shelagh said, in her breathy little voice, looking hopefully at her mother.

"All right," Kathleen sighed. "Just one."

Shelagh skipped the length of the bar, took her one crisp from Liam Keaveny's bag, thanked him, then brought her treasure back to Tom. "Bite, Grandpop?"

Tom pretended to nibble, while Shelagh giggled—clearly this was an established ritual. Shelagh looked up at Maggie, then silently held out her chip. Maggie mimed breaking off a piece and putting it into her mouth. As she patted her stomach, she had the satisfaction of hearing another round of giggles.

"I have a friend named Maggie," Shelagh said, a tiny bit shyly. "Maggie Durcan. She lives in Union Hall. Her cat just had kittens, and we're to get one. They're orange. I think orange cats are lovely, don't you?"

"I certainly do," Maggie answered. "I have one, in fact. Back home in New York. This big. His name—are you ready for this?—his name is Abraham de Lacey Giuseppe Casey Thomas O'Malley. I have a picture of him upstairs in my room."

Shelagh clapped her little hands. "That's a lovely

name. Only I should have ever so hard a time remembering it. I should like to call ours Marmalade, though Denny says he wants to call it Tiger." She leaned right up against Maggie's barstool, all traces of shyness gone. "Will you take me upstairs and show me your picture of O'Malley?"

"I was just going to ask you that myself," George murmured from behind Maggie.

"I didn't know you were interested in cats," she managed to tell him with a straight face, Shelagh forgotten for the moment.

"Oh, yes. So soft, so warm, so touchable—"

"If you two mean to get to Skib before the chemist closes," Kathleen said to her father and daughter, "you'd better be going."

"Grandpop, we can go!" Shelagh pulled Tom toward the street door. She waved to Maggie. "I'll let you hold Marmalade," she called out.

"You seem to have made a hit," George said. "You know, Emerald Eyes, I have a hunch a daughter of yours might look a lot like Shelagh."

"She's a darling child," Maggie exclaimed, trying to hold back a tidal wave of feeling.

Finishing off his drink, George said, "Easier to think about other people's children than your own, eh? Of course, a busy career as a New York journalist doesn't leave a lot of time, does it?" Before she could reply, he said, "Let's go."

"Go?" she echoed. "Where?"

"I want to scout locations. There's a glorious old stone ruin called Castle Killashee that I've dreamed of filming. Kathleen, they haven't razed Castle Killashee and built a motel there, have they?"

"That's the way you do things in the States," she retorted, "but here we have respect." She took down a beer mug, silently polished it with a soft cloth, then said to George, "I'm not so sure as it's clever to film there."

"Why on earth not?"

"Oh, you know how it is. There are folks think it's a sacred place."

"Sacred!" George laughed. "Kathleen, you're not going to tell me that Castlecove has gone cultish. Dancing to the wee people by the light of the full moon, and all that."

"It's not good manners to mock people's beliefs," Kathleen said, all tease gone from her voice.

"But, Kathleen," George persisted, "this is the twentieth century." Something in his face stopped her, and he leaned over the bar and asked, "You?"

"Don't be daft, George. It's just, you know, some people going overboard about being Irish. Teaching the old language in the schools, and making much of the myths."

"Why the fuss over the castle, though?" George asked.

"There's a fairy circle nearby, do you remember, and Killashee means 'church of the fairy hill.'"

"It's a beautiful name," Maggie said. "Sounds like wind blowing through leaves."

Offering Maggie a hand down from her perch on the barstool, George said, "Wait until you see it. Let's go."

How irritating of him simply to presume her willingness to go, Maggie thought. But she did want to see Castle Killashee. She calmed her pride by murmuring, with mock humility, "As you will, my liege. Lead me to yon castle."

She earned a wry half-smile from George and a nod of sisterly approval from Kathleen. Then Kathleen clapped hand to forehead in the classic gesture of dismay.

"But Dad won't be back for a good hour, and Bryan's all busy with dinner. Who's to take you?"

"I remember the way as if it were yesterday," George said. "You go up the road past Jimmy Fortune's store, then you take the turn for Leap, and you keep going up past the Hayes farm, minding not to run over their blasted old gray donkey, and then it's there on the left."

Liam Keaveny mumbled something from his end of the bar, the first words he'd addressed directly to them.

"Excuse me, Mr. Keaveny, what did you say?" George asked, with an elaborate politeness Maggie had never before heard from him. Again she had the unsettling impression that Liam Keaveny made him very tense.

"I said, the Hayes's old gray donkey is no more, so you needn't squander your curses."

Kathleen said to George around her grin, "You mean to drive yourself?"

"Did you think I'd gotten too grand to put my hand to a steering wheel?"

"When you called and said you meant to hire my dad for the month—" She broke off and shrugged.

George laughed. "Oh, that was mostly so I could give Maggie a cuddle in the back seat on the way down from Shannon. Very obliging, your dad was. Hung his cap over the rearview mirror and let us carry on like anything. At least, *I* carried on. Emerald Eyes slept through it all. Can you imagine?"

Outrage boiled up inside Maggie. At the same time, she had to suppress a shudder of excitement at the thought that George might be speaking the truth. But—impossible. Genevieve Joyce had been on the other side of George, no doubt keeping a sharp lookout from beneath her thickly mascara'd lashes. Maggie fought the temptation to rebuke George and turn on her heels, remembering just in time her resolve to put him down with teases instead of tirades.

"Some things just aren't worth waking up for," she lilted, with a pretty little yawn. "Ho, hum." She'd logged enough hours at the theater to know she'd delivered an exit line, and she started for the door.

"Dinner's at seven-thirty," Kathleen reminded her guests. "We've the first artichokes from the garden for a starter, and Bryan's had a joint of lamb marinating these three days."

"Oh, you women," George sighed. Pretending meekness, he followed Maggie.

chapter 11

THE RED-HEADED JOURNALIST from New York and
the dark-haired filmmaker from California walked out
into the late afternoon. They were greeted by beauty
so stunning it silenced all speech. The blue of the
harbor had grown a full tone more intense. The patch-
work green hills were radiant in the still-strong sunlight. Fuchsia bloomed abundantly in the foreground
of the vista. The soundscape rang with birdsong and
the scattered shouts of children at play. As they started
down the road to the van, it seemed to Maggie that
even the crunch of stone beneath their feet was a kind
of music. The fire-engine red of the van had clearly
been designed to create a magnificent clash with the
bluer red of the fuchsia.

Maggie sent up a brief prayer of thanks that she

lived in a time when jets existed, when women were free to adventure. Her silent joy intensified as they drove up a curving, hilly road, past Fortune's grocery store, made of lemon yellow stone, and a lime edifice with the name Fallon scripted over the dark green door and a big ceramic fish hung out by the name like a flag. They came to a black and white post laden with pointed signs: Glandore and Skibbereen off this way, Castlecove back the way they'd come, Leap to the left, and Rosscarbery to the right. One name was more poetic than the next, Maggie thought.

"I still haven't seen Castlecove," she realized aloud, as George took the Leap road. "The town, I mean."

"You certainly have. Well, all except for the petrol station. That's back down the other way, just across from the harbor."

"But where's the post office? Isn't there a church? Where does Bryan buy his lamb?"

"Molly Fortune—Jimmy's wife—is the postmistress. I'll take you by later and introduce you. The church is in Leap. Skibbereen's the big market town for this part of Cork, though it seems to me there's some butcher in Rosscarbery that Máire Farley favored, and maybe Bryan does the same. Most of the locals make do with dry goods from Fortune's, and maybe a bit of fresh fish from Fallon, and for eggs they go to the Hayes farm. Make their own bread, if they can't get to Ross or Skib and can't stomach the packaged stuff at Fortune's. Grow their own carrots and turnips or buy them from Kathleen."

"That sounds wonderful," Maggie rhapsodized. "Though day in, day out, it doesn't leave you much time for anything else."

"No, you won't find a lot of women journalists in Castlecove," George drawled.

"That's the second time you—George! Slow down!"

A few yards up ahead, a shaggy, stocky donkey the color of an animal cracker was wandering out onto the road, right in the path of the car. Her mocha foal came ambling out to join her from the adjacent field, as though the road were just the place for a leisurely chat about life.

Laughing, George stepped on the brake, and pulled over to the shoulder. "That damn literalist Liam Keaveny! He told me the Hayes's old gray donkey was gone, but he didn't tell me there was a new she-donkey in its place, and I do mean its place. That's exactly where the old one would come wandering out. This one's cuter, anyway."

"You met Liam Keaveny the first time you were in Castlecove, didn't you?" Maggie asked. "But he didn't seem very friendly." Instantly she regretted the comment. What she could only describe to herself as a look of pure misery crossed George's face.

"Oh, Emerald Eyes," he groaned. "Ten years is a long time to carry a grudge, isn't it? I was only nineteen. A damn fool, but not a scoundrel, no matter what anybody tells you."

"Oh, I'm the only one who's allowed to say nasty things about you," she said lightly. She was bursting with curiosity, but the wound was clearly too painful to be probed. No doubt George had indulged in some silly bit of womanizing—probably nothing too outrageous by American standards, but offensive to the people of Castlecove.

"Affectionate, aren't they?" she said, pointing to the nuzzling donkeys. "If anyone asks that mother if she's hugged her kid today, she can certainly say yes."

"Have you kissed your director today?" George teased, wholeheartedly joining in the change of subject.

Astonishing herself as well as him, Maggie leaned over and kissed him full on the lips, then fell back against the seat. If she kissed him again, she thought, she would have to spend the rest of her life kissing him, hopelessly addicted. "Kathleen's artichokes," she said weakly.

"Of course," George said. "We mustn't be late for Kathleen's artichokes. It's wonderful how you manage to keep your priorities straight." He tapped impatiently at his horn, but the donkeys didn't budge an inch. Sticking his head out the window, he yelled sharply, "Hey, Sadie! Get back to the farm."

She was the one he wanted to yell at, Maggie thought unhappily, as he started up the car again. She kept her eyes on the scenery. "Is that Atty Hayes's farm?" she asked, to thaw the chill, as they drove past a stone farmhouse and pasture land.

"Atty Hayes! Where did you hear about Atty Hayes?"

"I heard Tom Farley tell Kathleen he wasn't yet as old as Atty Hayes's goat."

His sharpness gone, George laughed. "He did say that, didn't he? Oh, Emerald Eyes, you can be funny. It's an expression, that's all. Like saying someone is as broad as a barn. Well, I suppose there's a bit more to it than that." George shifted down to take a steep hill. "Let's see if I can remember how the story goes. There was a Cork man named Atwell Hayes in the late eighteenth century, and he had a goat that lived on and on. When it finally died, Hayes's great-grandson served it up as venison on some state occasion, and everyone raved about good it was. Something like that. The Hayes who owns that farm is Seamus. Might be a descendant of Atty's, though."

Maggie looked at him, thinking how different he seemed now that they were in Ireland. It was as if the stage Irishman had stripped off his mask and costume only to reveal that he had a true Irish heart.

"You seem so at home here. You know so much

about the place," she said. "I know you brought me along to be your hairshirt and complain a lot, but am I allowed to compliment you once?"

"As long as you don't make a habit of it."

"Ireland becomes you. I can see why you made your finest film here. I really have great hopes for *Art O'Leary*."

To Maggie's astonishment, he looked less than pleased. "I thought you were going to tell me you liked my eyes," he sulked, and she wasn't at all sure he was joking. "At the very least, that you liked the way I handle a car."

"Doesn't it make you happy that I admire your work? Do I sound too much like a groupie?"

"A groupie!" George exclaimed. "Hardly! The whole point with a groupie is to get into the revered one's bed, not into theoretical discussions about his art."

"I'd have thought you'd had enough of that," Maggie said tartly, forgetting her vow to keep the talk frothy.

"Oh, sure," George said. "It's really irritating to have a beautiful woman whom you desire want to go to bed with you. I'm very tired of it. Thank you for sparing me." He pulled the van over to the side of the road and turned off the ignition. "We're here. Almost here. It's a bit of a hike." He looked down at Maggie's sneakered feet and added, "I should have warned you to put on boots. I'll drive up if you like. Or carry you, though I doubt you could stand my touch for that long."

No, I couldn't, Maggie thought, *but not for the reason you think*. "I don't own boots," she said. "Not hiking boots, anyway. Never mind. If I can walk two miles of New York City sidewalk in high-heeled sandals, I guess I can walk across that field in sneakers."

She followed him through a break in a dry stone

wall, up a narrow, rocky path. To either side lay
tangled grass splattered with the yellows, violets, and
whites of tiny wild flowers. Once again the beauty
of Ireland seemed to pull her out of her blue mood.
She swore that she absolutely, positively would refrain
from sparring with George, no matter how much he
irritated her.

"It's gorgeous here," she said, to make peace.

Seeming as eager as she for an end to battle, George
said immediately, "Isn't it?"

The path curved abruptly, and up ahead, through
a dense stand of yew and alder trees, Maggie glimpsed
the ruins of a massive construction, brown and crum-
bly looking, with great gaps in the thick walls—more
gaps than walls, really. The patchy blue sky served
for a roof. Air made the doors and windows.

She shivered. There was something so destroyed-
looking about the place.

"Creepy, isn't it?" George commented cheerfully.
"That's what I like about it. The perfect visual translation of Eileen's emotional ruins." He let his voice
go soft. He began to recite Eileen's opening words
in the *Lament for Art O'Leary:*

> "My love and my passion,
> "The first day I saw you,
> "At the market-house,
> "My eyes called you handsome,
> "My heart called you home.
> "I left all others for you
> "And followed you to far-off places."

He held out a hand to Maggie to help her across
a pile of broken stones blocking the main threshold.
A family of birds took sudden flight, and Maggie
looked up to see a nest lodged in a crevice. She walked
across a floor of dirt and grass and weeds and rubble.

She knelt to look out a low, rectangular window. She leaned against a wall and let her gaze wander where it would—to a fragment of cloud overhead, to a branch of alder growing in through a window.

"Eileen," a voice called out—George's voice. She looked around, but she could not see him. "Eileen," he called again, and she went to a window. She still could not see him. A small anxiety flared in her.

"George?" she called out.

"Here I am," he answered merrily, right behind her.

She whirled around. "You scared me."

"All in the service of art, Emerald Eyes. You were perfect. Eileen O'Leary come to life, flitting around looking for her husband's ghost."

"There's nothing about a ghost in the poem," Maggie protested.

"Not spelled out as such, but the whole poem's addressed to him, isn't it, and you just know Eileen thinks he's hovering nearby, hearing every word. Or hopes he is. Or wishes he were. Do you think you could search around again, the way you just did? I could block out the whole first scene in my mind. You were over there in that corner, then—"

"I know where I was," Maggie said. A little wave of excitement ran through her. She was actually going to help George MacDonagh block out a scene for what might turn out to be his most important film. "Are you going to get those birds to take flight again, too?"

George rewarded her with his flashiest grin. As she crossed what had probably once been a magnificent stone floor, he called out, almost as an afterthought, "Could you say Eileen's lines, too? Just that opening passage? 'My love and my passion'—"

"Yes, I know how it goes," she said quietly. "I read the script a dozen times on the plane. It's so beautiful, it just sticks in the mind. I always thought that was a mark of a great poem, that you remembered it without any effort. But is it right? I feel as though I'm poaching on Genevieve's territory." She felt herself flush as she realized the presumptuousness of what she'd just said. "Wouldn't she mind, you know, having someone stand in for her?"

"Oh, she'd die a thousand deaths," George laughed. "If she had to watch you, that is. But in fact Genevieve's the kind of gut actress who's nearly always best on the first or second take. So the more rehearsing I can do with a stand-in, the better off we all are. Of course, if you think I'm overworking you, just say so."

Maggie gave him the silent glare his remark merited. She paced the length and breadth of the ruined castle, peering searchingly about, letting Eileen O'Leary's beautiful lament fall from her lips.

> "My love and my passion,
> "The first day I saw you,
> "At the market-house,
> "My eyes called you handsome,
> "My heart called you home.
> "I left all others for you
> "And followed you to far-off places."

"Keep going," George rapped out in staccato tones. "Do you know the next part? 'I was never sorry'—"

Maggie looked out through a fragment of window at alder leaves stirring in the breeze. She looked at the jagged swath one wall was cutting across the bright sky.

> "I was never sorry.
> "You gave me everything.
> "Painted rooms for me,
> "Baked loaves for me,

"Slaughtered beasts for me.
"I slept softly
"In our feather bed
"Until midday milking time,
"Or later if I pleased."

She closed her eyes against the pain of the loss she suddenly felt. He had done everything for her, he had been everything to her, and now he was gone. Or was he gone? Out there, near the path to the road, she heard more than the wind in the trees. She heard something like his footstep, that merry footstep, that cocky scarperer's tread. She heard the voice that never trembled, not even when the English soldiers tried to bring him to heel. She heard him call out:

"My soul and my delight,
"I did not mean to leave you.
"I rode out that day
"Thinking only
"Of how coming home would be."

Her heart swelled. She called back:

"My love and my friend,
"Rise up from where you lie
"And let me lead you home.
"I shall make our bed
"With linen sheets
"And finely woven blankets
"To warm the precious body
"Which lies so still and cold."

Then suddenly he was stepping across the threshold as he had so many times before, his dark hair sweeping over his forehead, his pale eyes electric with desire, his arms stretching to embrace.

"My soul and my delight," he whispered tenderly, as he folded her up against him.

A thousand warning bells screamed in Maggie's mind. A thousand mufflers silenced them. "Please—" she began.

"Shhh," George whispered, and the whisper turned into a kiss, gentle at first, then insistent, then fiery fierce, until lips bonded to lips, and there was no world beyond Castle Killashee.

She did not resist. Could not. It was her own insistence he was meeting and matching, her own ferocity. She clung to him with all her might, as though to ease her hold for an instant would be to lose him again, and forever.

They sank to the rough ground. It would be their linen sheets, their fine embroidered blankets; desire would transform all. His hand splayed her rich red hair across the pillow of weeds.

"My friend and my love," he murmured. He caressed the planes of her face, again and again, as though to memorize them, as though to leave her with the indelible memory of his touch. If this was part of his plan for revenge, she thought wildly, let him spend an eternity getting even with her. Her body was a molten thing as his hands went to the buttons of her green and white checked shirt. He stopped, searching her eyes for permission. Oh, the very devil he was, making her give agreement for her own undoing. But she gave him the unspoken yes he was waiting for. There was no choice. Her powers of self-preservation were swept away in the wake of a longing a hundred times more fierce than anything she had known before. She lay almost faint beneath him as he undid her buttons with exquisitely torturous slowness.

He did not touch her breasts, and she knew what he was doing—letting the breeze caress the tender flesh that was rarely exposed to the elements, as a prelude to the caresses that would come from his hands. She moaned in pure sensual delight, then the breeze was no longer lover enough, and she felt herself straining toward George. Instantly his hands came home to her, anticipating every longing, creating new longings in her. She could scarcely believe that only one man was touching her, so wildly did his caresses vary—one moment gentle to the point of reverence, the next moment nakedly hungry and demanding. But then, she was only one woman, and she wanted everything that was coming from him—the naked hunger no less than the exquisite gentleness.

"Hey, in there!" The harsh voice came from the trees beyond, blasting them out of their idyll. "This is no place for carrying on, so."

Maggie's mind reeled sickeningly, and her body all but screamed in revolt, as George pulled her to her feet, putting protective arms around her. "Who's that?" he called out into the shadows.

"Never you mind who it be. Just take off, now, and no harm'll come to you."

Shivering, trying to get her buttons buttoned, Maggie felt as though she'd been deluged with ice water.

"We have every right to be here," George shouted angrily. "This is public land."

"It's hallowed ground, and we don't want Americans despoiling it."

"Let's get out of here," Maggie whispered. "He might have a gun or something."

"Don't be silly. This is Castlecove, not Forty-second Street. I want to know who it is. Maybe you can throw him off guard in a way I can't. Say something that will goad him into showing his face."

Thinking fast, Maggie tried, "We're making a movie here." She urged jauntiness into her voice. "We were just rehearsing. We're going to hire a lot of local extras, you know. Why don't you let us have a look at you? Maybe you could be in it."

For a moment there was only the sound of the wind in the trees, then the voice asked suspiciously, "What kind of movie?"

"A movie about Art O'Leary," Maggie answered.

"I don't see any cameras."

"We've just started rehearsing. The filming comes later." Her fear was gone; she was almost starting to enjoy herself.

"We'll see about that," the man said enigmatically. That was the last they heard from him. A few minutes later they saw a figure emerge from the path near their van, take up a bicycle, and ride up the hill.

"Wow," Maggie breathed. Her body was a mass of raw nerves.

"Indeed."

"I hope he won't mind about the movie. Was I wrong to tell him? That we plan to shoot it here?"

"Not for a minute," George said. "You almost had him ready to do a screen test, I think. In a day or so, everyone around here will know about the movie, anyway." He rubbed his hand across Maggie's cheek in that way he had and picked a twig out of her hair. "I just wonder how he knew we were here."

"Rode along and saw the van, I suppose."

"Maybe." George put both hands on Maggie's shoulders, then let his hands drop. "I suppose we should be going," he said reluctantly. Hand in hand they started down the path. "You know," George commented, "you're not a half-bad actress, Emerald Eyes. You really had me convinced back there."

Maggie felt as though she'd been punched in the stomach. Her mouth went dry. "Oh?" she managed to say. She rooted around in her mind for the sort of snappy comeback Kathleen would make. "It's easy to act," she said, with greatly overstated gaiety, "if you've got a great director guiding you."

"You really do think I'm up there at the top of the heap, don't you?" George asked, puzzling Maggie with the moody look on his face. Was it possible that there was a layer of insecurity beneath his arrogant exterior?

"I wouldn't be here," she said, "if I didn't rank you with the greatest directors." Still burning from his comment about her acting, she added loftily, "I didn't have to travel three thousand miles to get kissed."

"Hardly," he said brusquely. "I'm sure the lips were lined up around the block back home."

Neither Maggie nor George could keep a straight face thinking of lined-up lips, but the moment of comic relief quickly evaporated, and they drove back to Castlecove Inn in wary silence.

chapter 12

"TAKE THAT, GEORGE MACDONAGH!" Maggie shouted angrily, picking up her copy of the *Art O'Leary* script and flinging it across the room. It hit the director square on the side of the head, but he didn't stop grinning. Maggie's eyes darted around the room for more objects to throw. A ceramic ashtray, her traveling alarm clock, a pillow from her bed, a translucent Belleek pitcher full of garden flowers—all came to hand, all found their target. Finally George's grin died down. Finally Maggie's rage was spent.

Well, almost. Yelling and hurling within the confines of her mind could do just so much to calm her. A festive dinner, with George at his wittiest and most charming, had only intensified the pain and anger she'd felt earlier when he'd accused her of faking her passion for him. "You're not a half-bad actress, Emerald Eyes." The words seemed to reverberate off the peach papered walls. Actress! How could he have?

Did he really think she'd been faking? Did that mean he'd been faking? Lord, no, it just wasn't possible. Their sweet, sultry interlude had aroused her and moved her far more than any other intimate encounter in her life. If the faceless intruder hadn't shattered the heated moment, there was no telling how far they would have gone. No—untrue. She knew perfectly well how far they would have gone—to the other side of the moon, to the place where "stop" was not a part of the language, and love was the only law.

Actress!

Impossible. George was too smart really to have thought she was just getting into the role of Eileen O'Leary, clothing herself in Eileen's remembered lust for her dead husband. He was a professional. He was the consummate director. He knew who was acting and who wasn't.

Realizing that anew, Maggie felt all the more outraged and depressed. If he hadn't thought she'd been acting, then his comment could have had only one purpose—to hurt her, to goad her into losing her temper, to humiliate her. At the very moment when she'd begun to think that maybe, just maybe, she'd somehow misconstrued the words she'd overheard in the back of Tom Farley's car, he'd proved out her awful theory. He'd brought her to Castlecove to get even with her for having knocked him off his high horse at Sardi's, for provoking him into storming away from the table.

She'd cheated him of satisfaction, though, hadn't she? She'd been bubbly as champagne during dinner, and later had escaped from the strain of acting by announcing that she had work to do, and marched to her room. Then again, she had to admit, he'd cheated *her* of satisfaction. He hadn't come knocking at her door with some bright little line about taking up unfinished business. Was anything more frustrating than having the perfect rebuff ready and not getting a chance to use it?

She gave a huge sigh and turned the pillow under her head. Then she rearranged herself on the big, old-fashioned brass bedstead. Closing her eyes, she saw George MacDonagh, coming toward her with arms ready to embrace.

This wouldn't do. She sat up, looking over at the alarm clock which she'd had fantasies of flinging. Just after midnight here meant it was just after six in the evening in New York, and on her body clock. No wonder her mind refused to shut down. She wondered what the gang at *Limelight* was up to. She pictured her friends covering typewriters, getting ready to wander over to Joe Allen's for a drink, pairing up to go to the latest must-see Off-Broadway play. She hoped Tracy Nichols would remember to stop by the apartment and feed O'Malley and water the garden before she set off on her rounds.

Yawning, Maggie knew she had to find a way to get to sleep. She would need all her energy tomorrow. There would be a hundred little details to take care of so she could get down to being a proper publicist. She had to rent a typewriter and investigate copy shops; write up biographies of Genevieve Joyce, cinematographer Adam Manski, and George (damn him!) for the Irish papers; shoot off the first press release to the American media; and she had to make herself available—professionally, at least—to Larry Delgado. Then there would be a new member of the production company to get to know—Candy Kinicott, the daughter of an attaché at the American embassy in Dublin, who was driving down in the morning. Maggie had also promised to make signs announcing an open casting call for supporting roles in *Art O'Leary*, and to persuade merchants in Skibbereen to post the signs.

Maggie got out of bed and walked to the windows. Night was finally here, after a sunset that had lingered for hours. The long summer days and incandescent evenings were one of the splendors of Ireland, George had proclaimed at dinner, as proud as if he owned the country. Sometimes one even saw the northern lights. Yet the coast of Cork was warmed by the Gulf Stream. There was an island not far off shore that was famous for its palm trees.

Even looking out the window conjured thoughts which did anything but hasten sleep, Maggie realized with a sigh. Once, when she had been in her Greenwich Village apartment talking on the telephone to George in his Malibu beach house, the director had waxed poetic about the size of the stars as seen from Castlecove Inn at night. The stars were out there now, all right, and as big as advertised, but where was the loving embrace George had hinted at?

A soft knock sounded at the door. Maggie froze, then a smile played across her lips. So he'd come, after all. A shudder of excitement raced up her spine. She quickly rehashed her plan. She'd play along with George, and then, just when he thought he had her, she'd deliver the telling line, the body blow. "That was fun, darling, but you forgot to show your good profile. Do keep that in mind tomorrow. Now I must catch up on my sleep."

"Just a minute," she called out for real, pulling on panties, a pair of jeans, and a green turtleneck jersey that did nothing to conceal the absence of a bra. She hastily sprayed Shalimar cologne into her red hair.

She opened the door.

"Hi," said Larry Delgado.

"Hi," said a crestfallen Maggie. She felt an irrational surge of anger at George MacDonagh, as though he'd manipulated her into thinking he was knocking at her door, and now was laughing at his little joke.

"You sure know how to put out the welcome mat, Devlin. You going to invite me in?"

She hesitated. Larry Delgado had been perfectly correct in his behavior toward her since they'd landed on Irish soil, but she hadn't forgotten his midair change into a grabby lecher. Then again, he looked utterly domesticated in his old-fashioned pajamas with piping around the collar and a plaid robe and soft slippers. No man went philandering in slippers, did he? "Come on in," she sighed.

"Devlin, I don't know how to ask you this," he began, as he closed the door.

"Yes?" she said tentatively, wondering if she'd made yet another error in judgment.

"You don't happen to have a package of Oreos with you, do you?"

Maggie burst out laughing. The powerful movie critic, the internationally known maker-and-breaker of careers, had the woebegone look and voice of a nine-year-old boy, never mind the balding head. "You're kidding," she said.

"I'm starved," Larry declared plaintively. "I should have asked George to wake me for dinner. I'll never make it through to breakfast. I know, I know, it wouldn't kill me to lose a couple of pounds, but does it have to be tonight? You smell delicious. Like a vanilla milkshake. Do you have an extra elbow I could eat? What was for dinner?"

"Oh, nothing special," Maggie deadpanned. "Just artichokes from Kathleen's garden, and a joint of lamb that was marinated with fresh rosemary then grilled over a wood fire, and earthy tasting new potatoes, and a ruby lettuce salad, and trifle with cream so thick you practically had to cut it. You didn't miss a thing."

Larry groaned. "Tell me you're kidding. Tell me you really had lamb stew with flecks of congealed grease floating in it."

"That's not the way they cook in Ireland any more. At least not around here. Bryan Dunstable trained at Cordon Bleu in Paris, didn't you know?" Larry looked so shattered that she took pity on him. "Kathleen and Bryan did say we should just make ourselves at home, right down to raiding the refrigerator. They've gone to bed, but if you can figure out where the lights are in the kitchen—"

"Listen, Devlin, if I could figure out Brian De Palma's last two movies, I can figure out the lights. Lead on."

They tiptoed down the corridor, past the closed doors behind which George MacDonagh, Genevieve Joyce, and Adam Manski presumably slept, and into the kitchen. There were no other guests at the moment, and Kathleen had let Maggie know that the presence of the *Art O'Leary* company was a financial godsend. Castlecove Inn was developing a reputation as far away as Germany and France for it's sumptuous family style lunches and dinners, but the tiny village was off the tourist track, and, in Kathleen's words, people ate and ran.

"Devlin," Larry said, showing no desire to run after finishing a dozen cold slivers of Bryan's marinated lamb, "I don't believe this. I'm going to have to go straight from Castlecove to the fat farm, but who cares?" He looked over the stainless steel kitchen with its sixteen-burner professional range. He ran admiring fingers around the rim of his plate, a reddish clay circle partially covered by an off-white glaze, the plate obviously hand-thrown and hand-painted. "Four stars all around, no question. I wonder who made these plates. And the glasses," he added, hefting a goblet full of creamy milk.

"The plates were made by Stephen Pearce, who works in Shanagarry, about two hours from here. His brother Simon is the glassblower. He works up in Kilkenny. George said they're the leading young craftsmen in the country." Maggie smiled, proud of her knowledge of Ireland.

"And what George says is truth itself, right, Devlin?"

"Phillip Pearce, their father, is a great potter, too," Maggie went on blithely ignoring the barb. "His work is slightly more formal. A black matte glaze instead of the rough red clay that Stephen likes to show. Kathleen and Bryan used some of each at dinner. The two styles mix beautifully. And there were gorgeous woven placemats and linen napkins on the table, all Irish. I felt almost as if I were eating in a crafts museum."

"Let's drive up to Shanagarry sometime," Larry said. "I'd like to buy some of this pottery. I think my wife would really go for it."

Maggie felt herself relax a notch, almost as though a physical weight had been lifted from her. Sipping milk instead of scotch, Lorenzo F. X. Delgado seemed very definitely to have abandoned his free-lance Romeo role. Slippers, talk about his wife—the man was turning into a veritable lamb.

Maggie found herself saying, "Maybe I'll buy some Pearce pottery, too. And some Simon Pearce stemware. I had a complete set of wedding china and crystal, but I left it behind when I moved out of my husband's apartment. It always seemed too formal to me. John wouldn't be able to see the beauty and the elegance in this pottery. He—" She broke off abruptly. Larry might have turned into a lamb, but that didn't justify Maggie's getting into intimate subject matter, relaxing her standards of privacy. At this rate, she'd soon be telling Larry that once she'd ceased to be

John Venable's secret love and had become his wife, she'd found John too formal in bed, as well as in his taste for flowered china.

"What is it that makes me want to rattle on to you about my personal life?" She smiled to cover her abruptness.

"Probably the same thing that makes people rattle on to you, Devlin. We're both reporters, good ones, and the essence of that noble calling is being a good listener, the sort of listener people simply want to bombard with words. Which reminds me, tomorrow we've got to figure out the most efficient way for me to file copy. Send Telexes from the post office in Skibbereen, I expect." He spooned the last of the cream from his dish of trifle.

"It's on my list of things to do," Maggie answered him. "Let's clean up. I'm starting to feel sleepy, thank heaven. You want to wash or dry?"

"How about I sing you Cole Porter songs and you wash and dry?" Larry suggested hopefully. "Seriously, Devlin, the last time I caught a football, about ninety years ago, I fumbled it. You wouldn't want it on your conscience that this beautiful pottery got broken."

"The Dunstables let their kids eat off it, even the two year olds, so I don't guess it's any too fragile." She tossed Larry a dish towel. "Come on. It's five minutes' work."

Larry sighed. "I bet no one ever tossed George MacDonagh a dish towel, Devlin. Should I lose those ten pounds? Get a hair transplant, maybe?"

Maggie impulsively kissed the top of Larry's balding dome. "I love the way you look. You look like a newspaperman. You remind me of Sardi's upstairs bar at six, with all the reporters from *The New York Times* bending the old elbow. It's a mind transplant that you need. Women are tired of cleaning up while men sing to them, haven't you heard?"

"You can tell me all about it when we drive to Shanagarry."

"Okay. It's a date. Now dry, will you, please?"

Maggie was returning the stainless steel sink to the spotless condition in which she'd found it when she heard a door open upstairs.

"I think we've got company," Larry said, as the stairs creaked.

With awful foresight, Maggie knew that the company was certain to be George. She hastily put down the sponge she was using and untied Kathleen's yellow oilcloth apron advertising Colman's English mustard, but she couldn't undo the cozy domesticity of the scene.

"Well, well," George drawled, in just the tone she'd expected him to use. "How sweet. Playing house, you two? Hope you don't get dishpan hands. Might hurt your performance at the typewriter."

Staring wordlessly, Maggie thought that his appearance was really comment enough, his words salt in the wound. He was barechested and barefoot in his Levi's—clearly a man who hadn't owned pajamas, robe, or slippers since he outgrew sleep-away camp.

"I just came down for a fix," he said, going to the refrigerator. "You know how we Californians are, addicted to the juice of the orange." He took two oranges out of the refrigerator, looked at them disdainfully, and took out two more. He rolled them on the counter, pressing down as he rolled. "Makes them juicier, you know."

"We have oranges in New York, you know," Maggie said, mimicking his tone of voice. It was hardly the grand rebuff she'd planned earlier, but it would do for the moment.

Rummaging in a cupboard, and then another, George said, "You two should be dead with jet lag. What kept you up, a passionate discussion of Antonioni's use of close-ups? Maggie's very high-minded, Delgado, if you haven't already figured her out. Get her talking art—that's the way to do it. Ah, here it is," he added, as he found a squeezer, the old-fashioned green glass kind that always made Maggie nostalgic for her childhood.

"You know what you are, MacDonagh?" Larry said, throwing down his dish towel. "You're a sore winner."

Maggie wanted to hug the balding reporter, but she wasn't about to be so self-revealing. George merely raised his eyebrows and said, as he cut the oranges in half, "Nice line. A quote from one of your reviews?" He went to the cupboard where the Pearce stemware was kept, and took down two miniature goblets.

Two! Maggie stared at the glasses sitting on the counter next to the squeezer. Orange juice for *two* Californians. The second one *could* be for Adam Manski, but the likelihood, the sickening likelihood, was that the second glass was for Genevieve Joyce. Oh, Lord. She remembered that in the early days with John Venable—the thrilling, illicit days before they'd married—one or the other of them would go to the refrigerator for orange juice after they'd made love. Sometimes they would make love again, their kisses sweet and sticky.

In the front hallway of the inn, the telephone rang. Maggie, Larry, and George looked at one another, games forgotten.

"Who can it be at this hour?" Maggie asked. "A wrong number, I bet. I'll go get it before it wakes everyone up." She ran to the hallway. "Castlecove

Inn," she said courteously, just as she'd heard Kathleen do.

A man's voice, low and slurred with drink, rapped out a brief, horrifying message. "How can you sleep, woman, with the man who was the ruin of Nora Keaveny under your roof? Only sixteen, she was. Tell George MacDonagh some of us haven't forgotten." There was the click of disconnection, followed by the chasm of an open line.

Maggie saw Larry, ever the reporter, looking at her with curiosity. George was on his way up the stairs with a glass in each hand, but she would have sworn he was all ears. "I'm afraid you've got the wrong number," she managed to say into the telephone, despite the nauseating thuds of her heart. She hung up, turned out the light, and preceded Larry up the stairs, as though nothing had happened at all.

chapter 13

AWAKENING NEXT MORNING to the delicious smell of frying bacon and sausages, Maggie all too soon remembered the midnight telephone call she'd intercepted. The clear light of day did little to help resolve the turmoil that had been her uneasy lullabye and the prelude to a nightmare-ridden sleep.

The midnight caller had obviously been too boozed up to realize that Maggie, not Kathleen, was at the other end of the wire. Was she duty bound, then, to tell Kathleen about the call? She supposed she was, yet she felt deeply reluctant. The information was sure to bring anxiety to the hard-working proprietress of Castlecove Inn, and to what good end? Kathleen wouldn't be able to identify the caller from Maggie's description.

Tell George about the call, then? Every fiber in Maggie's being resisted that idea, too. To tell him would bring one of two responses:—either he would tell her what had happened between him and Nora Keaveny, or he wouldn't tell her. Maggie didn't know which would be harder to take.

"Only sixteen," she said aloud, bitterly. She'd thought she'd seen George's womanizing at its worst. She'd harbored hopes that his rakishness was part put-on, a role invented for him by his former publicist, Harriet Mills, a role he'd begun to believe in too fully—but no. Even ten years ago, when he was only nineteen, he'd apparently already regarded women's hearts and bodies as playthings. How had he wooed poor Nora Keaveny, Maggie wondered. What had become of her?

Keaveny. Keaveny. The dour solitary drinker in the Castlecove Pub the previous afternoon was named Liam Keaveny. Had that been his voice on the telephone at midnight? And what about the faceless intruder at Castle Killashee? Were they all one, or three different men? They were of the same place, and roughly of the same age, but Maggie hadn't been there long enough to distinguish voices heard only briefly, and at a remove.

Maggie's head began to ache. She needed coffee. For an instant she wished she were staying in some large, impersonal hotel and could go downstairs to a breakfast anonymously served among strangers. As she tucked a plaid man-tailored shirt into her jeans, she couldn't help remembering George's hands at the buttons of the green and white checked shirt she'd worn the day before. For one terrible, beautiful moment, she stood locked in leftover ecstasy, unable to move, to breathe. Then, exerting all her will power, she pulled herself out of the spell and prepared a casual, cheery face.

Walking into the dining room, she realized that luck was with her; she would be able to eat breakfast by herself, and not have to call on her dubious acting skill. The one person she encountered was Colleen Quinn, the shy teen-age daughter of the local physician, and the Dunstables' only helper at the moment. Colleen set a pot of steaming tea at Maggie's place, whispered that she was the last guest to descend for the morning meal, and fled back to the kitchen.

Normally an avid coffee drinker, Maggie decided after one sip that she loved Irish tea. It was aromatic and full-bodied, and seemed to have the wonderful property of dispelling clouds from the brain. Colleen reappeared with fried eggs, bacon, and sausage just as Maggie was pouring her second cup.

"Oh, no," Colleen declared, shocked out of her usual shyness. "You must never drink it without milk, 'twill destroy your stomach lining." She boldly doctored Maggie's cup, then took off before Maggie could tell her she couldn't possibly eat so huge a breakfast.

Again Maggie surprised herself. The Irish bacon, leaner and sweeter than its American counterpart, almost like fried ham, disappeared as though an invisible mouth were helping Maggie to consume it. The fresh flavor of the eggs made her think she would never again be content with the American supermarket variety, which always tasted faintly of carton. Clearly the last of the egg yolk demanded that the gently spiced sausage be dipped in it. Then, to frame the meal, she simply had to have just one piece—just two pieces—of the whole-grain bread called brown cake, with just a little bit of golden butter and just a tiny touch of Kathleen's homemade thick-cut orange marmalade.

Afterwards she sat staring in amazement at her empty plate. Not only had the milky tea banished her headache, and the breakfast gone down with unparalleled appetite, but her mood had turned almost sunny. Though the ominous midnight telephone call and the spectacle of orange juice for two still loomed large in her mind, she felt a sudden, inexplicable certainty that everything was going to work out. She was in Ireland, and George MacDonagh was about to begin filming *Lament for Art O'Leary,* and her troubles were what her Uncle Pat would call "of no more account than a drop of rain in the sea."

She glanced at her watch. She had a date to drive to Skibbereen with Tom Farley and little Shelagh Dunstable, but she had a good half hour until they were due to leave—time for a brisk walk. What with the Guinness and the sausage and the cream and the bread, she was going to have to be weight-conscious for the first time in her life. She could actually *feel* her jeans, and it was no use blaming her laundry for shrinking them. Castlecove was deliciously, dangerously calorific.

As she started up the curving, hilly road that eventually led to Castle Killashee, a car came whizzing her way. The driver held up a hand in greeting as he passed Maggie. She waved back. That small greeting between strangers struck her as beautifully emblematic of the part of the world in which she found herself. If only connections could always be so simple and sweet! Then again, one could hardly draw emotional sustenance from waves. The human psyche craved intimacy, with its rough-and-tumble as well as its sweet side. Why was it, Maggie rued, that the sweeter the sweetness for her, the rougher the roughness? The rest of humankind didn't seemed doomed to live in such extremes of emotion. Probably if she got to know the driver of the car just gone by, and started to like him, it would be no time at all before she was raging at him as well.

A powerful engine revved in the near distance, and

Maggie saw a silver sports car zooming toward her. Two cars in five minutes—a traffic jam by Castlecove standards. The driver, a young woman with racing goggles over her eyes and blonde hair flying, offered no salute as she sped past Maggie. Seconds later, Maggie heard the powerful car go into a racing change, stop, and back up. The car swept up the hill on Maggie's side of the road, so close that she was fanned by the breezes. Still the driver made no acknowledgment of her existence. Maggie kept on walking up the hill, only to see the silver car head toward her yet again. This time the driver ground to stop opposite Maggie. She stuck her head out the window, and Maggie saw that the blonde was no more than seventeen or eighteen, with a fine-boned face screwed up in a pout.

"Where the hell is Castlecove?" the young woman snapped at Maggie, in tones that all but accused her of concealing the village. "Up at the top of the hill there's a sign pointing down the hill, and at the bottom of the hill there's a sign pointing up the hill, and no sign of Castlecove in between."

She was an American, by her voice. Maggie didn't know whether she wanted to spank her or hug her. The blonde was very clearly a superbrat, not high on Maggie's list of character types. But her rudeness to a perfect stranger made Maggie more charitable toward herself. At least she only snarled at her friends.

"You're in Castlecove. This is it," Maggie told the young woman. "The two stores up ahead, and the inn and the petrol station back this way—"

The blonde didn't let her finish. "The inn. That's what I want."

"Right down there about half a mile. The big white rambling place with the red roof. There's a sign, actually, but it's hidden by the fuchsia." Maggie looked at the blonde and produced a smile to cover a sudden sinking feeling. "I bet you're Candy Kinicott."

"Damn straight." Candy Kinicott pushed her goggles up into her hair. "Who are you?"

"I'm Maggie Devlin. I'm George MacDonagh's unit publicist."

"Oh, yeah. I heard about you." Candy sized up Maggie with a brief, impassive stare. "You want a ride down to the inn?" she asked, in the tones of one offering the greatest of favors.

"I was going up to Fortune's, but...all right. Thanks." Maggie suddenly felt she wanted to be there as a buffer for Kathleen Dunstable when this snooty young thing announced her presence at the inn. She got into the car and settled back into the black leather bucket seat.

Candy ostentatiously stroked the grainy wood of the dashboard. "Nice old truck, isn't it? It's an XK-140. Jaguar," she added, making it clear that she considered vintage sports cars out of Maggie's ken and class. "My reward for getting into Vassar."

"Congratulations," Maggie said drily, wondering if Vassar College had recently lowered its standards or if Candy Kinicott had more substance than she showed on first glance.

"I had it up to a hundred twenty miles an hour on the road down from Dublin," Candy giggled. They maneuvered down the hill toward the inn at what Maggie considered an alarming speed—at what Maggie knew she was *meant* to consider an alarming speed.

"I believe you!" Maggie stared at the wildly fluctuating tachometer and prayed.

Candy downshifted, creating a great racket. "Are you sleeping with George?" she shouted casually, as if she were inquiring about the recent weather. "That's what your generation says, isn't it? 'Sleeping with'?"

Maggie threw a mock geriatric tremor into her

voice. "Do you mean, my child, am I keeping company with Mr. MacDonagh? Land sakes, girl, you young folks are bold as brass."

The joke fell flat. Candy announced impatiently, "I don't like to poach, but it's important to me to have him. He's worth ninety-two points, did you know that? Mick Jagger is down to a ninety, and even Eric Knightsbridge is only a ninety-five, and you know how hot he is."

"I thought that kind of groupie stuff was finished now," Maggie commented mildly. "The points and all that."

Candy tossed her long, buttery hair. "That's like people saying rock music is finished. There are always types who love writing obituaries. Don't worry," she added condescendingly. "I'm not interested in a relationship with George. He's kind of ancient for me. Anyway, I have a neat boyfriend back home."

"Lucky fellow," Maggie gushed, "having such a loyal old lady. That's what your generation says, isn't it? 'Old Lady'?" She groaned inwardly. No wonder the elder Kinicotts had been so quick to volunteer their daughter as production assistant when George called them to announce his trip to Ireland. She would hardly be an asset in diplomatic circles. Maggie just hoped that the blonde snobling played down her star-chasing in front of the Dunstables and other locals. Unfortunately, she thought bitterly, George would no doubt be all too delighted to help Candy score her ninety-two blasted points. Maggie wondered if he would chose Castle Killashee as their trysting place. Candy didn't look the type, though, to like twigs in her hair. A rendezvous by night in the star-strung garden, then? When Genevieve Joyce was asleep?

"There's the harbor," Maggie said, as much to break her own dark mood as to illuminate Candy Kinicott. "Isn't it something?"

"Not half so dramatic as the Ring of Kerry," Candy sniffed.

"I haven't seen Kerry, but it's much rougher, isn't it? Real cliffs? Not cultivated like these hills? That's the beauty of Castlecove, I think. Nature hasn't been tamed, exactly, but it's as though there's a truce between man and nature. Look at the dry stone wall twisting up there, between the pale green patch and the really dark green patch. Just plain stones, made by the ages, but they've been given form and meaning because human hands have arranged them."

"Very poetic," Candy sneered. "Is that a quote from one of your press releases?" She screeched to a halt in front of the inn, scattering stones into the fuchsia.

As Maggie had feared, Candy snooted Kathleen and Bryan Dunstable, just as she'd snooted Maggie. She asked to have the "bellboy" retrieve her luggage from her car and didn't crack a smile when Kathleen, deadpan, said that the bellboy had just run off with the manicurist. She barely acknowledged Tom Farley, who gallantly swept off his cap to bid her welcome.

Kathleen picked up on Maggie's displeasure over Candy's arrogance, and took her aside. "Don't worry, Maggie," the dark-haired sprite laughed. "I won't blame America for that cheeky young thing. I've dealt with her type before, so. I just wish Bryan and I could have her working in the kitchen with us for the summer. We'd soon show her what's what. My mother made a man of George the summer he worked here, and if he wasn't just a big, overgrown baby when he came to us, I don't know who ever was."

"I didn't realize he'd worked here," Maggie said. "That must be why he seems to know you and the place in a way no tourist ever could."

"Oh, yes. He worked the summer here. My parents

often did that, hired one foreigner as well as a local to help them out and be part of the family. That season we had George, and Nora Kea—" Kathleen bit the name off. She shook her head. The cherries in her cheeks were the neon red of maraschinos. "I was only fourteen," she said hurriedly. "I had a great big crush on him, I can tell you. He was about ten times as tall as I. Still is, though, isn't he?" Suddenly she reached out and touched Maggie's elbow. "Never mind what some folks say. Narrow, they are. Think Dublin is the other side of the moon, let alone the States. George is a grand lad underneath it all. My mother adored him. She never had a son, you see. But I musn't stand here gabbing away at you. Are you going into Skib with my dad? We're fresh out of biscuits for tea. Would you please ask him to pick up some Cadbury Chocolate Fingers and Jacobs' Ginger Crisps? Bryan swears by those, and two or three other packages, whatever he fancies. And if you can keep Shelagh from eating the half of them on the way home—"

"I can't promise to say no to Shelagh," Maggie laughed. "Ask anything else of me."

The two women's eyes met. Maggie's laughter died down. For one unsettling moment she would have sworn that Kathleen was just waiting for Maggie to pitch the sixty-four dollar question: *Who is Nora Keaveny? What happened between her and George that fateful summer?* Lord, thought Maggie, what a relief it would be to ask the question, to give up the lonely secret of the midnight telephone call. But to indulge in sordid gossip about George would be to put herself in the same class as Candy Kinicott. Worse—if she pitched the question, Kathleen might just toss back the answer. And if the answer was what Maggie suspected it was, she wasn't sure she could face George again, even as his publicist. She owed it to posterity to see that the film got made, and got made the way it ought to be made, right? *Right,* she answered herself, and went off in search of Tom Farley and Shelagh.

chapter 14

OUTSIDE THE GRAND French windows of the Castlecove Inn drawing room, the rain was streaming down.

"I'm glad for your garden," Maggie declared to Kathleen, "but I do hope it stops after lunch so we can begin production on schedule."

"That's Maggie for you," declared George MacDonagh, coming up behind her just in time to hear her last sentence. "Doesn't think about anything but art. Never mind if the grass withers and dies and the sheep have to eat last year's shoes. Just so long as the camera can roll."

Before Maggie could produce the right little acid bit of froth, Kathleen retorted, "If you're not twice a fool, George MacDonagh, I don't know who is. It's not as if we've had the drought this season, knock wood." She fervently tapped the mantelpiece over the great fireplace. "Now I'd better be seeing if Bryan wants a hand with the lunch."

"What got into her?" George began, but Maggie had already turned her back and begun to move across the room. She didn't feel compelled to answer. She sneaked a look at her watch. Almost one o'clock. Kathleen and Bryan had invited a dozen people from Castlecove and the surrounding towns to meet George MacDonagh and company at a buffet lunch. Maggie knew that Liam Keaveny was one of the locals expected. If he didn't show up, Maggie thought with a rising tide of excitement, that might well mean he was the mysterious caller of the night before, mightn't it? Pretty thin evidence, she had to concede to herself, and not much she could do with it in any event. But being on the case made her feel less guilty about not having revealed the call to Kathleen.

An electrical current ran around the room. Genevieve Joyce was making her entrance. Looking every inch the Hollywood star of the pre-denim era, she sashayed into the drawing room dressed in a tight black bouclé sweater threaded with gold, and gold lamé toreador pants. Her black hair was teased. Her eyelashes were so thickly mascarae'd, Maggie wondered that they didn't sink under their own weight. Her perfume turned the air to essence of jasmine.

The actress crossed to George and embraced him, as though they hadn't seen each other in weeks. Arm in arm, they began to make their rounds of the room, greeting the guests. Much though Maggie hated to spoil her notion of George as a walking, talking ego, she had to admit to herself that he managed to project convincing warmth as he circulated among the Dunstables' specially invited guests.

He discussed Belleek and Waterford with Rose and Denis O'Leary, who that morning had cordially of-

fered to display one of Maggie's casting-call posters
in their fine Skibbereen shop. He chatted about salmon
fishing in the Bandon River and the art galleries of
Dublin with a handsome American couple, the We-
bers, who rented a house in nearby Glandore each
year. He talked about a disastrous incident involving
a bowl of soup, which incident was to be chortled
over these ten years later, with Doctor Quinn. He
traded opinions on the political future of Ted Kennedy
with Mrs. Durcan of Union Hall whose daughter was
to give a new orange kitten to Shelagh and Denny
Dunstable. And he commented on the nature of donkeys with Seamus Hayes, the farmer whose land
abutted the grounds of Castle Killashee.

"Now tell me this, George MacDonagh," Molly
Fortune said pertly. "How is it you plan to start filming
this very afternoon when we've only just posted the
notice about your needing actors?"

"We don't shoot in sequence, you see. For the first
few days we'll shoot all the scenes that happen just
between Eileen and Art, then we'll fill in the bits and
pieces. Everyone knows you run Castlecove, Molly.
Can't you get the rain to stop? Though I half hope it
doesn't. I might go up to the Bandon with a fly rod,
or drive over to the estuary at Rosscarbery. Have you
met my cameraman? This is Adam Manski. Adam,
this is Molly Fortune and Jimmy Fortune. I know you
hate amateur photographers, but Jimmy has done
some shots of the boats in the harbor that have to be
seen to be believed. Doctor Quinn—"

If Genevieve didn't radiate the same charm, at least
she kept smiling and refrained from the drop-dead
sarcasms she was famous for. The lunch was a public
relations person's dream, Maggie thought. And the
credit all went to the marvelous Kathleen and Bryan
Dunstable. She told them so afterwards.

"Oh, we just thought it would be some fun," Kath-

leen said modestly. "And it seemed a good idea to
have the people hereabouts behind the filming."

Maggie couldn't pass up that opening. "Kathleen,
is there local opposition to the film?"

Kathleen averted her eyes. "It's as I told you yesterday. There are folks here that are very possessive
of the castle. And there's one or two remember George
as a brash kid."

"He's still a brash kid," Bryan Dunstable said,
putting an arm around his wife. He grinned, but Maggie couldn't help wondering if the dark-haired inn-
keeper resented Kathleen's ancient self-described
crush on the director, even if it dated back ten years,
to when Kathleen was fourteen and George nineteen,
and had very clearly come to nothing.

"I noticed," Maggie began boldly, "that Liam
Keaveny didn't make it to lunch."

Was her imagination working overtime, or did the
Dunstables exchange an uneasy glance?

"He's got the rheumatism," Bryan said. "Not so
keen on coming out in the rain."

The man who never missed his evening pints, by
Kathleen's initial description of him, was deterred by
rain? That hardly made sense to Maggie. Surely someone who'd lived his life on the coast of County Cork
was as used to the rain as he was to the sun. But
Maggie could hardly press the point without saying
more than she wanted to say. She thanked the Dunstables again for the gala lunch, and went upstairs to her
peach color room.

She passed a pleasant twenty minutes transforming
the room into a neat little office. The vanity became
a desk, with her rented Smith-Corona typewriter sitting importantly in the middle. She arranged her
photo-copied stacks of pressure-sensitive mailing la-
bels. Little Shelagh had already volunteered for the
job of peeling them off their protective backing and

sticking them to envelopes. All Maggie needed to get going full steam as a publicist was for the sun to come out and shooting to begin so she would have the makings of her first press release.

Nature cooperated. The rain halted as suddenly as it had begun. The green world outside Maggie's window sparkled as if the sky had just let loose a myriad of emeralds, not mere water. The next thing she knew, Candy Kinicott was rapping on the door, calling out in officious tones, "Van leaves in half an hour. Van leaves in half an hour."

Maggie's heart clutched as Adam Manski negotiated the laden van up the narrow path that led from the main road to Castle Killashee. She was just glad that George wasn't in the van with them but was riding with Genevieve, in grander style, in Tom Farley's Mercedes.

"Ah," said Adam emotionally, as the great old ruins of the castle came into view. "What an eye he has, our George. So many doors and windows, so many *frames*. Is made for a movie, this castle." The spare young Polish émigré with the blond crewcut jumped out of the van and paced the perimeters of the castle, cupping his hands as if to see through the camera's eye, gauging the angle of the afternoon light spilling through the unruly trees.

George arrived, and the two men set about unloading the van. As George placed an aluminum reflector to each side of the main entrance of the castle, and Adam threw sandbags over the legs of the stands to steady them, they looked as excited as small boys up to some particularly glorious, inventive brand of mischief.

"I don't know if we're going backward twenty years, or forward twenty years, but I don't ever remember starting a production and feeling so damn free." George exulted. "It's as if all my life I'd climbed mountains with ropes and pitons, and this time I'm going to do it with my feet. Maggie, we've got to remember when we're doing the credits: 'Lighting by God.'"

Her laughter echoed his, and for one glorious moment there was nothing between them but soaring joy.

"Kiss me," George demanded, his pale eyes dancing. "Kiss me for luck, oh publicist mine."

"For luck," Maggie whispered. She stood on tiptoes and let her lips brush his. It was scarcely more than a butterfly kiss yet she felt it reverberate in every cell of her body.

"But I don't need luck," George declared contradictorily, "if I have you. Tell me I have you. Let me die of an overdose of riches, right now." He gripped her shoulders. "Let me know that I have you, so I can weave the knowledge into the film."

Maggie stood there, pinioned by his eyes as much as by his hands, unable to move, to speak.

Tenderly stroking her throat, George said, "You look especially beautiful today, do you know that? As fine a muse as a man could ask for. There's a kind of feverishness about you. Tell me you tossed and turned all night thinking about me."

Maggie closed her eyes, not wanting him to know how right he was, and how much anguish there had been in the tossing and turning. She felt his lips press hers, and his arms encircle her, and now she knew a different anguish—the fierce desire she could neither accept nor deny. Then, for a sublime moment, as he pulled her to him and their bodies strained against each other, she existed in a state of white heat that burned up all thoughts, answered all questions.

"Geo-orge—" Candy was striding toward them, her blond hair bouncing behind her. "Adam says he can't find the shoulder pod."

"It's in the Aer Lingus flight bag, with the extra

batteries," George said, one arm still holding Maggie close. "I put it into the van myself."

Candy stared at Maggie with unmistakable hostility. "Getting into the part, Art?" she twitted George.

"That's right," George answered equably. The young blonde turned on her heel and headed back across the stony ground toward Adam Manski. George whistled up his muse. He began:

"There was a young woman named Candy
"Whose feelings inclined toward the randy.
"But when she was—"

"Geo-orge! Genevieve wants you!"

Reluctantly, George let his hands drop from Maggie's shoulders. "Maybe someday we'll get to finish something," he sighed. He dropped a kiss on Maggie's nose.

She stared after him as he started off in his long-legged stride. For a crazy instant she wished he weren't so devastatingly attractive. No matter how sure she was at any given time that she'd found true north, and that it lay where George wasn't, he had only to steal a kiss, or beg one, and the needle on her emotional compass flickered wildly. This afternoon, dressed in a richly embroidered shirt, tight Levis, and handmade cowboy boots, which he saw as the modern translation of Art O'Leary's eighteenth-century finery, he was all but irresistible. Yet she had resisted him, hadn't she? That was the strangest part of all. She'd given him her lips but not the words he'd asked for. And if she had? Would that have meant everything or nothing?

A small bundle of energy with hair as red as Maggie's own was running toward her—Shelagh Dunstable. Bryan was coming up behind her with five-year-old Denny astride his shoulders.

"Mama can't come because the twins are sleeping, but she said we mustn't miss the action." The little girl clapped her hands. "It's so exciting."

Maggie grinned. "It is, is it?"

"I've seen two films, *Bambi* and *The Muppet Movie,* in Cork City, but I never thought I'd see a film in the castle."

"Darling, I hope you won't be awfully disappointed." Maggie got down on the child's level. "We're not showing a movie today, we're making one. Genevieve Joyce and George are going to pretend to be some people called Eileen and Art, and Adam is going to take pictures of them with that pretty blue camera—do you see it?—and there's something called a magnetic recorder that's going to pick up all their words. See Candy putting those big mouse-ears on her head? That's called a headphone, and it will let her make sure the sound is coming through. Does that make sense?"

Shelagh nodded vigorously. "Oh, .yes. You're a very good explainer. My mama and papa are good explainers, too. But do you know what Maggie Durcan's mama told her? She told her there's a piece of the sun inside light bulbs, and that's how they work. Isn't that silly? Because if they were full of sun, they wouldn't work at night, and that's when we really need them! I'm going to go tell Denny about the magic recorder."

"Magnetic," Maggie corrected gently.

Shelagh started to dash toward her brother and father, then stopped in her tracks. She looked wistfully at Maggie. "After they make the movie with the magic recorder, then will we see a film in the castle? I do hope it has animals. I think animals are lovely, don't you?"

"I do," Maggie said. She stared after the child, feeling some combination of love and longing she'd never known before. She'd always adored children in the abstract, but, aside from the occasional toddler she saw in a shopping cart at the A & P, little people scarcely seemed to cross her path in New York.

She pulled free of her mood and went to greet Bryan and Denny and the other local people who had come to see the filming get underway. She noted with satisfaction that Larry Delgado was talking with Seamus Hayes, the neighboring farmer, and Molly and Jimmy Fortune. Larry was taking copious notes. If the people of Castlecove thought they were going to be written up in the American press, they would be all the more eager for the production to go smoothly.

George and Adam signaled their near-readiness. Maggie ran down the path to post a big sign she'd made: FILMING IN PROGRESS—SILENCE, PLEASE. That would get the message across to any tourists who just happened to pick today to visit Castle Killashee.

As Maggie got back to the grounds of the castle, a black-clad Genevieve Joyce emerged dramatically from behind the van, crossed in front of the small knot of onlookers, and went to take her place just inside the jagged castle walls. Tom Farley began to clap, and applause rippled across the open space. George let the actress have her moment, then stationed himself next to Adam Manski. The cameraman raised the vaunted TK-76 to the cushioned pod on his right shoulder.

"Quiet on the set," George called out. Maggie felt an electric thrill dance through her body at the authority in his voice. History was happening now. George MacDonagh was about to film again.

Candy Kinicott, holding a slate on which was chalked SCENE ONE, TAKE ONE, positioned herself briefly in front of the camera.

"Speed," Adam Manski announced, signaling that the camera was rolling.

Genevieve Joyce paced the length and breadth of the castle, peering, searching. She knelt to look out a low window. She raised her eyes to the sky. Her face registered a vast range of emotions. There was infinite pain in her eyes. Yet pure joy wafted off her as she became Eileen O'Leary remembering other times.

> "My love and my passion,
> "The first day I saw you,
> "At the market-house,
> "My eyes called you handsome,
> "My heart called you home.
> "I left all others for you
> "And followed you to far-off places."

Maggie felt the words in her own mouth, the emotions in her own breast. Her fists clenched and her heart clutched as George MacDonagh—no longer a director but an actor; no longer an actor but Art O'Leary come to life—approached the castle in that cocky stride of his, his boots crushing twigs, his great lean height diminishing the very trees. He stood poised outside the broken walls, torn between the joys of announcing his presence to his love and covertly hearing his praises sung by her. Ego won out. He stood listening, his smile growing, as Genevieve—no, Eileen—relived the pleasures of their marriage bed. At last he spoke.

> "My soul and my delight
> "I did not mean to leave you.
> "I rode out that day
> "Thinking only
> "Of how coming home would be."

Not until his wife, his widow, called on him to rise

up and come to her, did he cross the threshold and let her see his face. Then—

No! Maggie had to clap a hand across her mouth to keep from shrieking out her anguish. He was looking at Genevieve, touching Genevieve, kissing Genevieve, pulling Genevieve down to the rough ground, putting his hands to the buttons of her shirt, stopping to seek permission from her eyes exactly, to the smallest detail, as he'd made his moves with Maggie the day before.

Oh, God, was there no end to the man's monstrosity? How could he have violated her this way, saying that he wanted to weave his feeling for her into the film, only to crudely expose their most intimate moments?

She turned and bolted from the horrifying spectacle. If he'd secretly photographed her naked body and exhibited the pictures, she couldn't have felt more abused, more betrayed. He had used Maggie's flesh, her emotions, her very being to hone his performance—*and everybody knew!* That was the most horrible part of all. She was certain everyone knew. Bryan, Candy, Larry, the Fortunes—all would look at her body and know that George's hands had caressed her breasts and the caresses hadn't moved him at all. The caresses that had redefined the universe for Maggie had merely been a rehearsal for George MacDonagh.

She sought refuge behind the van, on the far side, out of sight of the crew and the crowd, facing toward the Hayes farm. She watched the cows. Her eyes followed the lonely uphill journey of a woman pedaling her bike along the main road.

Maggie's mind swirled. Her body ached all over, as if it had been beaten.

She tried the old deep-breathing routine. She sank to the ground and arranged her limbs in the basic yoga positions. But she couldn't focus. Genevieve Joyce's throaty voice was projecting through the trees, crying out those passionate words again. Apparently George had ordered a second take. Maggie wondered if he'd really found the first take less than satisfactory, or if he just wanted the pleasure of publicly groping Genevieve again.

A car was coming up the road now, slowly, an old green Volkswagon. It was stopping, right where the path to the castle began. Maggie went on alert. She'd posted her sign asking for silence, but the castle was on public property, and there was no guarantee people would heed. The three big men getting out of the Volkswagon might even be tourists from a non-English-speaking country who wouldn't understand the sign. Too late, she realized she ought to have posted her plea in French and German as well.

Maggie started over toward the path. She would head the men off. She almost hoped they would give her trouble. She had rage to spare.

Then she heard one of the men's voices carry up to where she was. "Naked lovemaking," she heard him utter in loud disgust. "Americans despoiling our sacred places. We'll show them."

She stopped. She paled. She knew that voice. It was the coarse voice that had threatened her and George when they were locked in their torrid embrace in the castle. At least she'd thought it was a torrid embrace. If these men made it up the path and saw Genevieve and George going through the same paces, all hell might break loose. She had visions of a smashed camera, even of smashed faces. These men were big. And if the other two were as riled up as the one whose voice she recognized, they were riled up indeed.

She had to stop them.

She leaped into the van. She didn't dare turn on

the ignition because the sound might be picked up by the powerful Ampex 3000 recorder. She didn't have to. The nose of the van was pointed downhill, down the path, because Adam had turned it around to make unloading easier. As she released the brake and depressed the clutch, the big vehicle rolled straight toward the men. They saw the silent monster gliding toward them and jumped to either side.

"Turn around and get the hell away from here or I'm going to keep going until I smash into your car," Maggie hissed.

Her eyes focused long enough on the three startled faces to memorize their features. She heard one of the men yell, "Liam!"

They turned around, racing her down the path and yelling, and for the first time she realized there was a fourth man in the car. He heard the noise, saw the red monster coming, moved over into the driver's seat, and jerked the car out of Maggie's path and up the road. The three other men cut through the field beside the path and jumped into the car, which raced away.

Maggie coasted to a stop. She sat staring at the cows opposite, waiting for her heart to slow down, then looked into the rearview mirror, and grinned. Her red hair was sticking out every which way. She must have looked a right demon gliding down the path in the red van. Too late, it occurred to her that she should have gotten the license plate of the green car, but she wasn't sure it really mattered. She had a feeling those men wouldn't be any too eager for another round.

She didn't want to drive the van back up the path, in case the recorder was still on, so she pulled it well over onto the field and parked it, then got out and walked.

When she arrived back to the production site there

was a break on. Everyone was babbling about how great Genevieve and George had been in the second take, what a gloriously moving film it was going to be. Larry Delgado was feverishly scribbling. "Not since I saw Burton's Hamlet," he rhapsodized to Maggie, then went on writing. Adam Manski was caressing the blue video camera, as if they'd just made love together. Candy Kinicott was sitting on the ground, arms folded around her legs teenybopper style, looking generally transported. Maggie felt her adrenaline pumping in response to the excitement. But as she looked at George and Genevieve, huddled together on the threshold of the castle, she wished, for one anguished moment, that she'd let the three thugs destroy the production.

chapter 15

THE THUGS' SHOUTS had been heard, though not by the recorder. Maggie had to tell her story.

She was almost relieved. It would have been unbearable to be the guardian of yet another dramatic secret. The only difficult part was describing her own role. She hardly wanted to proclaim that she'd been a heroine. But she could have saved herself the worry. Candy Kinicott was eager to take her down a peg.

"I know it wouldn't have been as exciting," the blonde American teen-ager drawled, "but wouldn't it have been smarter to let the men come up here? If they're from around here, Bryan or Tom or someone would have recognized them. Adam might even have gotten their faces on film."

"You didn't hear them. I did," Maggie answered

quietly. "They were really angry. If Adam had aimed a camera at them, you can believe they would have smashed it to bits and destroyed the tape. And suppose they'd really hurt someone? Okay, we could have identified them in a court, but in the meantime the film would have been ruined and someone seriously injured."

To Maggie's amazement, Genevieve Joyce jumped in on her side. "Don't be euphemistic, darling. I'm the one they would have banged up, right? They always go for the female star, don't they? A nice little broken nose or some other disfiguring act? I, for one, am very grateful that you got them beforehand, even if it meant they got away."

"Terrible, terrible," Tom Farley muttered. "I can't believe anyone from these parts would do such a thing, so." His face was alarmingly red, Maggie thought. He wiped away a thick film of sweat.

"Who else but a local would know about the filming?" George mused.

"There were those signs you've been putting up about the casting," Molly Fortune pointed out.

"Yes, but those just went up this morning." George looked at Maggie. She averted her eyes. He hesitated a moment, then added, "I was up here yesterday, looking over the location. Someone came on heavy with me, about not wanting Americans around. I didn't say anything because I didn't take it too seriously, to tell the truth."

"Are you going to bring in the Guarda?" Seamus Hayes asked—a trifle anxiously, Maggie thought.

"I've never been a big one for going to the police," George grimaced. "Maggie, you really think they won't come back?"

She shivered. "Either that, or they'll come back a dozen strong, and armed."

Maggie knew she had to take George aside and tell him about the threatening phone call of the previous night. Yet to talk to him in private, especially to allude to his behavior with women, was more than she could face at the moment. Face it she must, though. She was in a state of delayed shock, she knew, and if ever she'd earned a moment's peace it was now. But how much responsibility for the safety of the production and cast could she take upon herself? Telling the truth about the call might give George the last clue he needed to solve the mystery and forestall the next threat.

Unless she confronted Liam Keaveny herself?

Her heart pounded at the thought. She was nearly positive he was the man at the wheel of the green Volkswagon. Virtually certain that Nora Keaveny was his daughter. Just about convinced that George's treatment of this Nora in the past was responsible for the hostilities of the present. But what if she was wrong? She might destroy an old man's fragile equanimity for nothing.

Hadn't George guessed that he and his production would be less than warmly welcomed in Castlecove? Why had he come back here? Yes, Castle Killashee made as breathtaking a film set as she could imagine, beautiful and terrible at once. But surely there were other magnificent ruins that would have done nearly as well.

She had to talk to George.

She gritted her teeth and started toward him. He and Adam and Candy were loading up the van. She watched the perfect fluid strength of the man as he heaved a fifty-pound Fly-A-Way sandbag.

Larry Delgado grabbed her by the elbow, causing her to jump a good two feet. "You know," the journalist declared, "if I weren't convinced you were one of the world's honorable women, Devlin, I'd think you cooked up these so-called thugs as a publicity plot."

"I don't know about how honorable I am," Maggie demurred, "but I'm afraid you're overrating my powers of invention."

"I think your powers of invention are just fine. Fine and dandy. You invented that wrong number last night, didn't you?"

He slid the question into the conversation so smoothly that Maggie had no chance to mask her reaction. She stood stonily quiet.

"Hey, come on, Devlin. I thought we were friends. You're not going to start playing the no-comment press agent, are you?"

"You're not going to start playing the investigative reporter, are you?" she parried. "You're a film critic, remember?"

"I started out on the city desk. Never quite got it out of my system. Who was that on the telephone last night?"

"Larry, I—" She broke off. Candy Kinicott had linked arms with George, who didn't seem to mind in the least, and was standing way up on tiptoe to whisper into his ear. George nodded and grinned.

"Terrific idea," she heard him say. Then he called out to Tom Farley. "Tom, why don't you take Genevieve back to the inn on your own? Candy's going to give me a lesson in how to drive the Silver Bullet." Almost as an afterthought, as if Maggie were some poor orphan he had to feed, clothe, and transport, he called to her. "Emerald Eyes, you can go back in the van with Adam. Think you can face the van again?"

Maggie repented of her next words before they were out of her mouth, but there was no stopping them. "Don't forget to let Candy hear that nifty little limerick you worked up about her," she snapped in a voice blazing with dislike. Too late, she realized that she'd slipped back into her old temperamental ways, letting everything hang out. She searched around in her mind for some lighthearted bit of nonsense. She didn't find it. She'd blown her cool and there was no un-blowing it.

To her astonishment—though how could anything astonish her now, she wondered—George took a step toward her, his pale eyes gleaming with something that bore a remarkable resemblance to tenderness. Larry must have seen it, too. He moved slightly away from Maggie, as though conceding George's prior claim.

"I thought you'd misplaced that temper of yours," was all George said. "I was starting to miss it."

Of course, thought Maggie, on a brand-new wave of misery. Part of his elaborate plan for revenge was to trick her into publicly venting her most private emotions. What a satisfying moment *this* must be for him—Maggie exposing her inner self in front of Candy Kinicott and Larry Delgado. It was so satisfying that he actually felt tender toward his victim.

She turned to the journalist with what she hoped were sparkling eyes. "Hey, Larry, how about that drive up to Shanagarry you suggested? I know it's late, but I'm full of energy after my little adventure. I bet if Kathleen called Stephen Pearce for us he'd show us his pottery, even if we arrive after his usual closing time." She crossed her fingers behind her back.

"Terrific, Devlin," Larry boomed, with even more enthusiasm than she'd hoped for. "I was sure you were going to back out. Who keeps promises made at midnight, right?" he added, with a lascivious wink that was just right. "There's a place in the hills overlooking Cork City called Arbutus Lodge. Great food and a fantastic view of the Cork harbor, according to a friend back in Chicago-town. The highest-rated wine cellar in Ireland, if I remember right. We can have a relaxed dinner there on the way back. I'll call and make a reservation after Kathleen sets things up with her friend the potter. Is Bryan still around? I want to talk to him about a car."

"He took the kids back to the inn."

George had stood still—frozen—during Maggie's exchange with Larry. Now he pushed the dark hair back off his forehead with an angry gesture that satisfied Maggie, yet pierced her, too. Candy Kinicott tugged impatiently at the director's arm. He hesitated, then said, "That's a lot of driving on unfamiliar country roads after dark."

"Devlin and I know our way around," Larry replied airily.

A panicky sense of foreboding filled Maggie. "Don't let me go!" she silently beseeched George. "Don't go off with Candy! Put an end to this madness. Let us make a leap together. It's what we're on earth for."

If George sensed her inner turmoil, he gave no sign. He turned and walked off with Candy toward her silver Jaguar.

Larry put a friendly arm around Maggie's shoulders as they headed for the van. "Did I do okay, Devlin? Help to turn El Genius's heart green with jealousy?"

"My feelings are that obvious?" Maggie sighed.

"Afraid so. Don't ever volunteer to be a spy, Devlin."

"You were pretty nice to play along. Lord, it's a relief to be able to talk straight for a change."

"Pretty nice!" Larry echoed indignantly. "I was downright magnificent. Of course I'm working my angle, too, don't get me wrong. What do you say we spend the night at Arbutus Lodge and really give the old boy something to be jealous about?"

"Larry, I can't. If that's the only reason you want to drive to Shanagarry, forget the whole thing."

"Don't tell me a woman with your enlightened politics believes in the double standard, Devlin."

Maggie stopped in her tracks. "What's that supposed to mean?"

"You don't think Candy and El Genius are just going off to talk about overdrive, do you?"

Maggie didn't answer. She pulled away from him and hurried stiffly toward the van.

A contrite Larry puffed after her. "I'm sorry. That was low, Devlin."

"My standards are my standards," she got out from between clenched teeth.

"I know. But that's not the point. Want the opinion of one of the smartest men you'll ever meet? George couldn't care less about Candy Kinicott. You're the one he's interested in."

"But it's a sick interest. He's obsessed with hurting me," Maggie exploded.

"Then why do you still care so much about him? Never mind, Devlin. I withdraw the question. There's never been a simple heart in the whole history of mankind—excuse me—personkind. Why should you be different from the rest of us? I hope everything works out for you. I really do. And let's just have a pleasant drive up to Shanagarry, okay?"

"You're on."

Back at the inn, they found that Kathleen had heard about the would-be attack at Castle Killashee and was extremely upset. She clucked over Maggie, and asked if she was really up to the drive to Shanagarry.

"All I need is a bath and a change of clothes. The drive will be the best medicine. Actually, Kathleen, it's those men in the green car you should be fretting over. I gave them a scare."

"I can scarcely believe it happened. Not that I doubt

you for a moment, Maggie, but the folk around here aren't like that."

"You did say there might be some hard feelings about us filming at the castle," Maggie pointed out.

"Hard feelings are one thing, and storming the set is another. And to think Shelagh and Denny were there, and might have got hurt!"

"I hope, by the way," Maggie said, "that Bryan wasn't sorry he'd brought them. Not because of the thugs, because of the—ah—love scene."

Kathleen waved her hand impatiently. "He said it wasn't any worse than things they've seen on the telly. They thought it was funny, I expect. It's the killing scene I wouldn't want them to see. Where's George, now? I think he should call the Guarda."

"He's off. With Candy." Maggie avoided the other woman's eyes. "And I'm off to the tub. Will you let me know if you get through to Stephen Pearce?"

On her way upstairs, Maggie impulsively stuck her head into the pub. Bryan was there, manning the bar; and the handsome American couple she'd met at lunch who came to Glandore so the husband could fish and the wife could paint; and two tourists drinking Guinness and toasting each other in French; but not Liam Keaveny, though this was his hour.

She stretched her long body out in a tub full of hot water, and sniffed the gentle spiciness of the Irish rose soap she'd bought at the chemist's in Skibbereen—a real luxury at ninety pence for the small, round bar, but worth every pence. She would wear her favorite midi-length wool challis skirt, she decided, and her dark green cotton rib-knit sweater, and boots, and bring a blazer against the cool of the Irish evening. Larry was being very decent. He deserved to have a glamorous woman on his arm.

For all the extra effort she put into her appearance, she was still ready fifteen minutes early. It was funny how no one ever seemed to be in a rush in Ireland. Her Uncle Pat had a favorite saying: "God made time, and plenty of it." She'd thought it was so much hokey Irish nonsense when she was moving in her normal New York rhythms, somehow compelled to zip along at top speed even when she was doing nothing at all. But here in Castlecove she seemed to be able to pack endless activities into a day without once hurrying. Maybe it was the belated sunsets that made each day feel like a miniature infinity.

She didn't want to hang around downstairs while she was waiting for Larry and risk running into George and Candy on the way in from their outing. She sat down in a flower-spangled over-stuffed armchair and picked up a book of poems, but two days in Ireland couldn't undo her New York compulsiveness, belated sunsets notwithstanding. She sat down at her typewriter and pushed up her sleeves. She might as well get a start on the press release she would want to send out tomorrow.

Castlecove, County Cork, Ireland, she typed at the top of the page. *For immediate release.* She paused, trying to think up a catchy lead, then a broad grin played over her face, and her fingers started flying across the keyboard.

George MacDonagh, the egomaniacal director, began shooting his latest film today on location at Castle Killashee.

The new work—MacDonagh's eleventh motion picture—is Lament for Art O'Leary, *based on an eighteenth-century poem written by Eileen O'Leary of Cork after her husband was shot by the British. The epic stars Genevieve Joyce and MacDonagh, who thinks he's as talented in front of a camera as behind it.*

The opening scene is a sexy clinch which should earn MacDonagh an R-rating—R for Ridiculous—

and cement his reputation as a man who never makes love in private if he can do it in public. The "love scene" will probably go down in history as one of the great unintentional comic passages on celluloid, MacDonagh, wearing the tight jeans and expensive cowboy boots that are his trademark, strides into the ruins of Castle Killashee as if he were making an entrance at a singles bar. He looks out toward the audience to make sure that every groupie's eye is fixed on him. Then, keeping his good profile to the camera, he all but throws Genevieve Joyce to the rough ground.

Some film buffs will insist that the scene is a deliberate parody of the torrid embrace in Gone with the Wind. *Others will simply say that MacDonagh should have stayed behind the camera.*

The camera in this case is an RCA TK-76. MacDonagh, who originally claimed that he wanted to make history by having cinematographer Adam Manski use video equipment, confessed today that he bought the RCA model mostly because it is blue, the color of his eyes.

She read the words she had just written. Too bad she couldn't really send it out. It would probably create a lot more interest in the film than a straight press release would. Oh, well. It had been great fun to write, and wondrously therapeutic, even if it would never reach the audience it deserved.

She read the fake release once more, chuckled her satisfaction, then rolled the paper out of her rented Smith-Corona, crumpled it up, and flung it into the wastebasket.

"So there, George MacDonagh!"

chapter 16

MAGGIE PRESSED HER face against the steamy window on the driver's side of the stalled Mini, and watched the rain cascade down. Nearly midnight, and they were still a good hour from Castlecove. Getting only a labored grinding noise when she turned the ignition again, she groaned aloud. The rain had clearly shorted out the electrical system, and there was nothing to do but wait for the storm to subside.

"I suppose you think it's my fault," she exploded irrationally, but Larry refused to rise to the bait. "You'd think a car built in Britain would be better able to handle rain," she went on, tapping her fingernails against the steering wheel.

"Relax, Devlin. We'll get there sooner or later.

How about a game of ghost? Or see who knows more Cole Porter titles? 'Why Don't We Try Staying Home.' How's that for an apt one?"

"Please, Larry. Please. Don't tell me to relax. You know I hate that. I just know they're getting frantic about us back at the inn." She stared out into the wet blackness, and listened to the beating of the rain on the roof. "If only there were some place we could call from."

"They're probably all asleep. And if they're up— it's most likely raining in Castlecove, too, and they've figured out what's going on. I bet Bryan's sat by the side of the road in this buggy more than once waiting for the rain to stop. It was a nice evening, wasn't it? Up until now, anyway?"

It had been a very nice evening, Maggie had to agree. She and Larry had been as taken with the affable, irreverent Stephen Pearce as they were with his pottery, and had ended up buying every single mug, plate, and serving piece either of them could afford. Dinner and the view of Cork harbor at the Arbutus Lodge had also lived up to their expectations.

That's why they'd gotten caught in the deluge, Maggie lamented. They'd let themselves have too good a time. She felt guilty, as though she shouldn't have enjoyed herself quite so much in the company of a man who wasn't George MacDonagh. Oh, the daft workings of her mind! Worrying that he was worrying, feeling as guilty as if she'd cheated on him. And all the while he probably wasn't giving her the smallest thought.

Who had rocked him to sleep tonight, she wondered grimly, Genevieve Joyce or Candy Kinicott? Or had he generously accommodated both ladies in the course of the evening? She wouldn't put it past him. She wouldn't put anything past him. And yet—

"I think it's slowing up, Devlin," Larry said.

Maggie cranked down her window a cautious two inches. The deluge was now merely a downpour. Then, as suddenly as it had started, the rain halted.

She turned the ignition. Still there was no action. "I guess we have to dry off the engine," she said. She felt strangely cheerful, now that there was action to be taken.

"What do you mean, dry it off?" her companion asked.

"Just what it sounds like. Take a cloth and go out there and get under the hood and mop up the water. Under the bonnet, I guess I should say."

"You're kidding, Devlin. Won't it evaporate by itself?"

"What, in the strong sunlight?"

Larry sighed. "I was just thinking how cozy it would be in the back seat. That doesn't sound very orthodox, taking a cloth to the engine."

"It's exactly orthodox," Maggie smiled. "I took a car repair course a couple of years ago. Now," breezily, "we just have to figure out what to use as a cloth. I think your shirt would be perfect. Pure cotton, isn't it? Very absorbent."

Larry patted the tiny alligator on his open-neck maroon sport shirt. "Come on, Devlin, this is a genuine LaCoste. What about your sweater? That's cotton, too, isn't it?"

"I guess anything is better than the back seat," Maggie returned spiritedly. "I'll take off mine if you'll take off yours. There's a lot of mopping up to do." In one sleek move, she turned her back, whipped off her green sweater, and pulled on her blazer. "There," she said, buttoning the three buttons and shrugging her shoulders to make the jacket fit just right. "Your turn."

"Oh, Devlin. As the great Porter put it, 'So Near and Yet so Far'." He cast one longing look her way, gave a huge sigh, pulled off his shirt, made a mocking display of a hairy but not exactly muscular chest, and reached for his trenchcoat. "I feel like a pervert," he grumbled, as he buttoned and belted the coat.

Sweater and shirt were sacrificed beyond redemption, but the mopping up did the trick. Maggie turned the ignition and the car leaped to life.

"I wonder if we should call," she mused, as they hit the outskirts of Bandon.

"Devlin, what's all this worrying? You must have grown up with overanxious parents. There's just that one phone out in the hall, remember. You'd probably wake the whole joint up if you called. It's El Genius you're worried about, isn't it? Believe me, it'll do him good to stew about you."

"It's one thing to have him wonder if we decided to spend the night at Arbutus Lodge, and another thing for him to worry that we may be having car trouble. Remember that comment he made about our being careful on unfamiliar country roads?"

"I don't remember. It wasn't one of his deathless quotable quotes."

"I just know he had a premonition and he's stewing," Maggie insisted.

"That's got to be the silliest thing I ever heard from a rational person. Premonition, Devlin? You're getting awfully California there. Next thing you know you'll be asking me my astrological sign."

They went on through Bandon in silence. Then, as they were crossing the Temple Bridge in Rosscarbery, Maggie said, "I'm getting sleepy. Sing to me, will you? Not just Cole Porter. I'm getting tired of Cole Porter. Johnny Mercer, maybe? Kay Swift? She's one of my favorites. Do you know 'Fine and Dandy'?"

"Kay Swift!" he exclaimed with mock anger. "She wrote our damn theme song, 'Can't We Be Friends'." He sang it, with a wry tenderness, and 'Fine and Dandy,' too, and all the other songs she wanted to hear. She joined voices with him, and by the time she parked the car between Tom Farley's sedate old Mercedes and Candy Kinicott's Silver Bullet, she forgot to worry about what George MacDonagh might or might not be doing, thinking, feeling.

She pushed open the front door that Kathleen and Bryan never locked. Instantly she heard a door open upstairs. A light went on in the upstairs hall. Looking as though he'd dozed off in his clothes, George came bounding down toward them.

"Maggie? Are you all right?" he began. Then the expression on his face changed, and he simply stared at Maggie's and Larry's peculiar state of dress. "You had to sell the shirts off your backs to get all the pottery you wanted?" he asked icily. He turned and started back up the stairs.

Maggie stood riveted, but Larry took the stairs two at a time and grabbed a fistful of George's shirt.

"MacDonagh, are you crazy?" he said in a hoarse whisper. "Our electrical system flooded. Then Devlin here had the brains to realize that the only thing to do was open the hood and mop up the water, and that's where the clothes went. You've forfeited the right to hear this, but Devlin ruined what would have been a terrific evening by moaning from Cork City to Rosscarbery about how anxious you were probably getting. I think you two nuts deserve each other." He let go of George's expensive denim and stalked off to his room.

"Well," said George MacDonagh.

"Well," said Maggie Devlin.

"So you know about cars, do you?" the director asked, with an expression she couldn't quite fathom.

"I know about everything," she said giddily, "except men. I mean, I wouldn't have expected Larry to do what he just did."

The dark-haired director and the red-haired writer looked at each other. Half a flight of stairs still separated them. The house made the sounds that sleeping houses make. The one dim light illumining them flickered, then held steady.

"Actually," George said, "I think you know a lot about this man."

"You mean knowing that you would worry tonight?"

"Not just that, though I did worry. For sure I worried. I was thinking—" He paused, as though to search his memory. "Egomaniacal. Never makes love in private if he can do it in public. R-rated for ridic—"

Maggie took a step forward, her fists clenched, her face white. "How dare you go through my wastebasket?" she hissed.

"Ah, the old offensive defensive," George said. "It never did much for the New York Giants, and it won't do much for you, Emerald Eyes. I suppose that, being the East Coast person you are, you don't believe in the unconcious, but why did you leave that piece of paper crumpled so invitingly in your wastebasket, and leave your door unlocked? Because you wanted me to see that document, maybe?"

"This is Ireland. People leave their doors unlocked. Kathleen and Bryan leave the whole house unlocked. Of course, not everyone in Ireland is Irish," she added, thinking about Candy Kinicott and her desire to win George's favor, probably at any cost.

"No," George agreed noncommitally, "not everyone in Ireland is Irish. But maybe the paper was found more innocently than you think. Never mind. That's rather beside the point, don't you think?"

A cold wind seemed to cut through the house.

Maggie hugged her blazer closer to her skin. "Am I fired?"

"Is that what you want?" George asked. "Is that why you wrote that damned thing . . . hoping I'd find it and send you packing?"

"No!" she burst out, unable to play games for another moment. "That's the last thing on earth I want!"

George looked at her so intensely that her knees began to shake. Merely to inhale and exhale seemed to require every ounce of stamina she possessed.

"I want to get this very straight," he said. "You want to stay on because you admire my work?"

"That's part of it—" she began.

His face lighting up with what could not be anything other than joy, George started down the stairs toward her. "Only part of it?" he repeated.

"Only part of it," Maggie said softly, knowing that she could no longer conceal her true emotions from herself or from George. She loved this man. If loving him were folly, then she would find a way to live with folly. But his radiant expression seemed to say that he wanted her to love him, that her fierce longing for him had not led her astray.

He stood in front of her now, not touching her.

Moved almost to tears by what she saw in his eyes, Maggie dropped her gaze. "I'm forgiven for the press release, then?" she asked huskily.

"Well, now, wait a minute," George said, causing her head to bob up in alarm. "I don't know if you can be allowed to get off scot-free. I think you should be fined."

"Fined?"

"One kiss for each offense," George said. "Does the defendant have any objection to the sentence?"

"No objection, your honor," Maggie murmured.

George moved so close that she could smell the clove-and-cinnamon scent of his dark hair—some all-natural California creme rinse, she guessed, feeling all at once oddly fond of things Californian. He moved closer still, so that she could hear the rhythms of his heart. Yet he did not put his hands to her, and she thought that at any moment she might die for want of his touch.

"For calling me egomaniacal," he intoned, "the penalty is one kiss." He bent toward her and, still not putting his hands on her body, let his lips brush hers. "For calling me R for Ridiculous, one kiss." This time his lips pressed hers, forcing her own lips to part, and she swayed and would have fallen if his arms hadn't finally gone around her. "For saying that I came striding into Castle Killashee as if it were a singles bar, one kiss." Now she could taste the sweetness of his mouth as his kiss grew more passionate, and she no longer knew where her lips ended and his began. "Is that all?" he asked, a beautiful eternity later. "Have I exacted proper penance for your sins?"

"Oh, no," Maggie cried softly into the warmth of his neck. "I made fun of your boots and jeans—" He kissed her. "And I said you bought the camera to match your eyes—" He kissed her. "And, oh heaven, I can't think of the rest, but I know there were dozens, hundreds—"

"Dearest, darling Emerald Eyes," he sighed, after an exhausting few minutes, "you'll wear me out if you don't mend your ways. On the other hand, please don't mend your ways. I want to go on fining you forever. Oh, Maggie, I fell in love with you the moment you knocked over that beer bottle at Sardi's. You do care about me, don't you? About me, the man, not just George MacDonagh, the director? Emerald Eyes, Emerald Eyes, until I read that press release, that awful, wonderful press release, I didn't dare hope. You seemed to care only about my art. If I touched you, you shied away as if you hated me."

"Oh, no," Maggie breathed, "it was just that I knew if I let myself go at all with you I'd have to let myself go entirely."

"Then I read those words," George went on, "and I knew how much it had stung you to see me touch Genevieve, and then, at last, I knew what I wanted to know."

Shuddering at the memory of the the scene at Castle Killashee earlier that day, Maggie said, "You didn't just touch her. You touched her the way you touched me. Oh, Lord, how that hurt." She stood looking up at him, arms wrapped around her chest for warmth, suddenly uncertain.

"Don't you see?" George implored. "I thought if I could get you to regard our kisses as the stuff of art, I could go on having those kisses. And I had to have them. How I've wanted you from the very beginning."

"But I don't understand," Maggie blurted. "I thought you only brought me to Castlecove to humiliate me, to pay me back for the way I behaved that day at Sardi's."

"Humiliate you? Never. I did want to pay you back, that's true. You handed me my head that day. Pretty painful surgery, but you saved my life. You got me back on the true course just before it was almost too late. And I saw you, totally committed to New York, to journalism, the way I'd got locked into Hollywood and big pictures, and I wanted to show you that there was more. I wanted you to see Ireland, and know you were connected with it, and that there was other work you should be thinking of doing."

"Publicity?" Maggie asked skeptically.

"No," George laughed. "You're damned good at it, as it happens, but I was thinking more along the lines of your writing your own movies. My own movies, I should say. Making art instead of just writing about other people's art. Maggie, I want to work with you. I want to do everything with you. I—" A sudden look of comprehension flashed across his face. "You little scamp!"

"What now, your honor?"

"You weren't asleep in the car coming down from Shannon. That's when you got the idea I wanted revenge, from the things you overheard me say to Genevieve."

"I didn't mean to eavesdrop," Maggie told him, shaking her head at the ghastly memory. "I would have given anything really to be asleep." The dark thought crossed her mind that parts of the overheard conversation had yet to be explained away to her satisfaction.

Then George was saying huskily, "I think it's time we went upstairs, don't you?"

Heart pounding she knew this was no moment for dark thoughts, or second thoughts. If nothing else on earth were certain, this much was—she and George were in love, and love had to rule the day. There was all the time in the world for worrying over each other's imperfections. Right now, to do anything but celebrate would be to show ingratitude to the kindly fates that had given them each other.

Suddenly George picked her up in his arms, all five feet, nine and a half inches of her, and carried her up the stairs, all the while whispering the words of love and desire into her hair.

"Your room or mine?" he asked at the top of the stairs.

"How about your room, then my room?" she replied, greedily, happily.

He tenderly arranged her on his bed, cradling her head with a pillow. She swooned as she caught the sweet, spicy scent of his hair on the pillowcase. He unbuttoned her blazer and slid it off, and she came out of her sensual haze to unbutton his denim shirt.

Feeling the naked strength of his chest against hers, she let down the final barriers in her mind. She knew now that when George possessed her, she would not lose herself but find herself.

His lips left her mouth to kiss her throat, her shoulders, the crook of an elbow—there seemed to be no inch of her body that did not crave his sweet kisses . . . crave all of him.

Afterwards he said, "Did I remember to tell you that you're the most beautiful woman in the world?"

Nestling contentedly in his arms, she murmured, "You mentioned it."

"Did I tell you I loved you?" George asked.

"Fourteen times, and then I lost count."

"Did I mention that I want to marry you?"

Maggie's breath caught in her throat. "No, actually. I don't believe you did."

"I would get down on my knees," George said, "but my knees seem to need a rest."

"Do save your knees," Maggie said, shakily. Her mind was swirling.

"I do love you so awfully much, Emerald Eyes. And you do love me?"

"Oh, George, I love you passionately. I love you in a way I've never loved anyone else."

"You'll marry me, then? We'll be the Devlin-MacDonaghs of New York and Los Angeles and Castlecove? Lord, how wonderful that sounds. This will seem crazy, I suppose, but for years and years I didn't understand why people married, and now I know. When we—"

Maggie put tender fingers to his lips. Grateful for the darkness, she mustered all her courage and said, "I love you, and I want to be your mistress, but, darling George, I can't, I won't marry you."

chapter 17

"IT'S BECAUSE OF the women in my past, isn't it?"
George said hoarsely. He sat up and fumbled on the
table next to the bed, then burst out laughing. "Seven
years since I quit smoking, and I'm looking for my
cigarettes, which should give you some idea of how
rattled I am. Damn it, I wish I'd never met one of
those women. Only—no. I'm not sure I'd really ap-
preciate you as much as I do if there hadn't been all
those near-misses. I don't hold your marriage against
you, darling. Oh, I'm a little jealous just because he
knew you when you were twenty, and I wish I could
have, too, but then, I'm jealous of your mother because she got to hold you as a baby. Look at that,
Emerald Eyes, my hands are shaking. My kingdom
for a Camel. Give me a chance to change your mind,

will you?" Drawing breath, looking at Maggie with frantic eyes, he suddenly coined one of his limericks.

"There was a young man from L. A.
"Who proposed to his true love one day.
"She said, 'I will bed you,
"But, sir, I can't wed you,'
"Destroying the man from L. A."

Maggie threw her arms around him, not knowing whether to cry or laugh, and ending up doing a little of both.

George kissed away her tears, then said, "You're going to have to let me muster my most persuasive arguments, though I scarcely know where to begin, since I never before tried to convince anyone to marry me. In fact, I had to convince a few people not to. Oh, damn, that was the wrong thing to say, wasn't it? Emerald Eyes, let's throw on some clothes and go downstairs and have a drink, and discuss this little matter. It's merely the future of civilization hanging in the balance, do you realize? Not just our personal happiness? If you marry me, and we have children, there it is, the world altered forever. Here, do you want to get back in your blazer and skirt, or shall I go to your famous unlocked room and get your jeans. See what a model husband I'd make? Fetching your clothes for you?"

As she lay there in the dark waiting for him to return with her jeans, Maggie hugged George's half of the pillow. Surely no more exciting man had ever lived—and he wanted her! And she wanted him, as she'd never wanted anyone else. But would marriage really be the glue that would bind them for eternity, or the end of their hard-won joy? Her mind flooded with old dreams—the hopes she'd had for marriage when she was a girl and a young woman. She knew that some people believed the "mature" way to approach marriage was with modest expectations, but if she didn't feel certain those old, cherished dreams had a chance of coming true, then what was the point of marriage? She didn't think she could survive another failure, least of all with her true love.

George came back with her clothes, and, barefoot and in denim, they tiptoed downstairs. The pub was long since closed for the night, but the hospitable Kathleen and Bryan had let their guests know that the private liquor cabinet in the drawing room was as available as the refrigerator.

Turning on lamps, George and Maggie heard a sudden sound of banging doors from the Dunstable family quarters.

"Oh, no, we've woken someone up," Maggie said, dismayed.

Tom Farley came weaving toward them in his long nightshirt, looking at first like a man who'd been startled out of a deep sleep, then looking somehow so terribly not-right that Maggie was filled with apprehension.

"Water," the gray-haired man mumbled. "So thirsty—" He stumbled toward them. "Máire!" he cried out, as he saw Maggie. "Where have you been, woman? You gave me a turn, disappearing that way. I've missed you something fierce, I have. There's been a spot of trouble, Máire. The old business about Nora. Should I tell them what you told me just before you went away? Why did you go, Máire? For God's sake, woman, give me a drink of water, I'm fairly perishing." His eyes rolled wildly. He fell.

"Tom!" Maggie sank to her knees next to him. "Go get Kathleen," she rapped out to the stunned George. "But try not to wake the kids. Shelagh mustn't see him like this. Hurry! I'll get something to cover him."

"Darlings! Whatever is going on down there?" Genevieve Joyce called throatily from the upstairs hallway. She theatrically drew a red silk kimono about her famous curves. "You could raise the dead with that racket. I need my sleep, you know, or I'll have circles under— Good God! What happened to him?" The actress leaned over the railing, then came hurrying down the stairs, just as Kathleen and Bryan were rushing across the drawing room with George.

"He's breathing," Maggie assured everyone. "His color's not too bad. I don't think it's a heart attack or stroke or anything like that." She'd grabbed coats from the front hall closet, and now she tenderly arranged them across the supine man's inert limbs.

Bryan got Dr. Quinn on the phone. "He wants to talk to you," he called out to Maggie. "Tell him everything."

Maggie tersely described Tom's appearance and actions. As she did so, she saw Genevieve clutch at her throat and grow visibly paler, than kneel at Tom's side. For all the terrible strain of the moment, Maggie couldn't help thinking that she'd never seen Genevieve look more beautiful, more compelling. If only this were a scene from a film, not real life!

Larry Delgado appeared at the top of the stairs. "Is it those thugs again?" he asked. "Was there a break-in? What's going on?"

All at once Genevieve came striding across the room toward Maggie. She reached for the telephone with an imperious gesture to which Maggie could only accede.

"Dr. Quinn? This is Genevieve Joyce. Tom is in a diabetic coma, I'd stake my life on it. I'm the wife of an internist who specializes in pancreatic disorders and an insulin-dependent diabetic myself, so I know what I'm talking about. Yes. Right. Good. Here's Kathleen."

A few minutes later Kathleen said that they were to take Tom to the emergency room at the hospital in Skibbereen, Dr. Quinn would meet them there, to save time. He was certain that the diagnostic tests would confirm Genevieve's suspicion. If she turned out to be right, they could all draw a great sigh of relief. Maturity-onset diabetes was easily kept under control by proper diet, exercise, and insulin injections. Tom would probably be out of the hospital in just a couple of days, as soon as the doctors had done all the work-ups and taught him to give himself the injections.

George insisted on driving Tom's Mercedes to Skibereen so Kathleen could sit in the back cradling her still-unconscious father. Maggie and Genevieve, who'd managed somehow to get on slacks, sweater, and mascara in two minutes flat, rode in the front with George.

"You were amazing, Miss Joyce," Kathleen said softly from the back seat. "Thinking so quickly, that way. I do pray you're right, and it's not something worse."

"I know I'm right," Genevieve asserted. "When I found out I had diabetes, I read so much on the subject my husband said I ought to get an honorary medical degree. That's how I met my husband, in fact. He's one of the leading authorities in the world on diabetes. Sexy way to get to know someone, isn't it?" She chuckled. "Our eyes met across the hypodermic needle, and we knew we were made for each other."

"Is it fearfully hard, learning to give yourself the injections?"

Genevieve sighed. "I've been rather a great big baby about that part, I must confess. Alexander, my husband, is a believer in what he calls the 'raised consciousness' for diabetics, being very open about it, even giving yourself the injections in restaurants if you're on a schedule tied to mealtimes, as I am. But I've got a *thing* about needles. And I am so awfully vain, you know. I've kept my little secret to myself, up until now. At home my husband gives me the injections, even though he grumbles about life with me being one long busman's honeymoon. And dear George has been forced into the role of needleman on this trip. Poor lamb, I even dragged him into the loo on the plane so he could shoot me up before dinner. Heaven only knows what people thought we were up to in there. Hello?" as Maggie, sitting between her and George, started violently. "Are you all right?"

"I'm fine," Maggie said faintly. "I just—I was just sitting on the seat belt buckle."

Maggie closed her eyes and leaned back, feeling a great tide of self-dislike wash over her. Lord, what a lot of trouble a suspicious mind and a hot temper could make for a person—for everyone. It was nothing less than shameful, disgraceful, that she'd leaped to interpret Genevieve's and George's words and actions the way she had. The tandem visit to the 747 lavatory . . . Genevieve's reference to black-and-blue thighs . . . George's comment about how much more comfortable it would be to "do it" in a room at the inn than in the back seat of the Mercedes. These had not been the adulterous little sex parties Maggie had imagined, but life-sustaining injections of insulin.

She wallowed in guilt as George urged the Mercedes through the night. Then she remembered, as though she'd seen the movie only yesterday, a scene from *Dublin Dreams,* her favorite of George's movies. "There are two kinds of guilt," an old woman told the hero of the movie. "There's guilt that does nothing except make you feel miserable, and then there's guilt that leads you to make reparations for the wrong you've done. Go. Make wrong right."

Maggie gulped hard, then said, "Genevieve, I think it took incredible character for you to give away your secret tonight. You know that Larry Delgado is going to want to capitalize on it, because what good newsman wouldn't? How can I help? I have to be honest and tell you that it goes against my nature to act as a censor, to be the sort of press agent who tries to keep things out of the press, but if that's what you want me to try to do, I'll do it. I feel I owe you, that we all owe you, and Larry and I are friends, so—" Her voice trailed off.

"That's very kind, darling," Genevieve drawled, "but it probably wouldn't work, would it? One whiff of pressure, and Larry would probably tell them to run the headlines twice as high. That's what I'd do, if I were a reporter and upholding the Right of the People to Know."

"I'm afraid I would, too," Maggie agreed unhappily.

"Darling, this is too nauseating," Genevieve suddenly laughed. "I do believe you and I are going to be friends!" A much-needed laugh ran around the car, and then Genevieve said, more somberly, "I've been thinking, you know. Dear Tom is going to want a bit of cheering up when he finds he's got diabetes, if indeed that's what he's got. He's not the type to like being ill, is he, Kathleen?"

"Never!" Kathleen exclaimed. "I've been thinking about that, too. No matter how mild it is, the man is that afraid he'll be a burden on me, and not be able to drive from here to there and back again every day. He won't take it lightly, so."

"Well, then," Genevieve declared, "you see? Clearly the time has come for me to go public. We'll have insulin parties, Tom and I, and let the scriveners write and the papparazzi photograph, we won't care at all. That would cheer him a little, wouldn't it, Kathleen?"

"Oh, Miss Joyce, you don't know. I daresay my dad would rather be diabetic than not if it meant he got to spend more time with you!"

"Kathleen, you're a dear girl. You must call me Genevieve, you know. I'm only a hundred and fifty years older than you." The actress yawned elaborately, happily. "I don't know what's wrong with me. You'd think this was a party. I seem to like the whole world. Well, almost the whole world. George, what *are* we going to do about that Kinicott creature? A troublemaker if ever there was one. Can't we send her out for coffee . . . to Colombia?"

"I don't know," George said, "Adam Manski seems to think she has great possibilities . . . on the set and off."

"Good luck, Adam," Genevieve said fervently. "You'll need it."

Maggie thought about a rifled wastebasket and silently echoed her words.

They were at the outskirts of Skibbereen then, and the mood in the car grew more serious. Kathleen mutely told George which turns to take for the hospital. Maggie felt her stomach knot as Dr. Quinn and two attendants got Tom Farley onto a stretcher and carted him into the hospital. Genevieve wasn't a physician, after all. What if she'd been wrong? What if Tom were in fact the victim of some truly dread affliction? Maggie kept thinking of little Shelagh, and how devasted she would be if anything bad happened to her beloved Grandpop. She'd recover, of course— children did—but would there ever again be that unalloyed delight in life?

Kathleen, George, Genevieve, and Maggie paced

the pale green waiting room—the eternal hospital waiting room, Maggie thought, interchangeable with a million others. Occasionally a nursing sister came through, but never with news for them.

What seemed an eternity later, Dr. Quinn appeared, his thumbs up. "The man is pure sugar," he exclaimed. "We've got an I.V. going with insulin. He'll be coming around any moment. Kathleen," he added, shaking his head, "this can't be sudden. He must have been feeling poorly the while. Why didn't you send him to me, lass?"

"You know my dad and doctors. I begged him only the other day to drop in at your office. And when you were coming for lunch, I tried again, even though it was a social call, so."

The doctor put a hand on her shoulder. "I didn't mean to sound as though I was blaming you. I suppose I'm feeling bad myself because I see the man more days than I don't, and I didn't put two and two together. He'd lost some weight and was hungry and thirsty all the time, now as I think on it." He tottered a bit, then looked at his watch. "Going for three. Why don't you go home and get some sleep and come back in the morning. You'll have your hands full, you know, getting the man to stick to his regimen, and keeping his spirits up, too."

"Oh, that's taken care of," Kathleen said, gesturing toward Genevieve, and explaining. "I'll just run and kiss him goodnight, then we can go on." She jumped up.

"Quite a young woman," Dr. Quinn declared, as she moved out of hearing. "Favors her dad in looks, I'd have to say. But in spirit she's her mother all over again. Máire would be that proud of her, I daresay."

The reference to Máire Farley brought back the highly charged moment in the downstairs hallway at Castlecove Inn when Tom Farley had mistaken Maggie for his dead wife, and cried out that "the old business about Nora" had surfaced again. Nora Keaveny, surely. Maggie let the name swirl around in her mind. Had she been as wrong about George and Nora as she'd been about George and Genevieve? One thing was absolutely certain—she'd been wrong to let fears about Nora and George fester within her rather than confront George with them.

As they were walking back toward the car, Genevieve put her arm around Kathleen, and started to give her a private little pep talk about Tom. Maggie decided that, for all the emotional overload of the last few hours, she'd better bring the name of Nora up before she lost the courage of her new convictions.

"Do you remember," she started, linking her arm through George's, "when Tom thought I was Máire, and he said something about a woman named Nora?"

"Maggie—"

"What, sweet George?"

"Nothing. I'm sorry," he said. "Go on."

She told him then about the anonymous telephone call she'd intercepted. "How can you sleep, woman," she echoed the whiskeyed voice, "with the man who was the ruin of Nora Keaveny under your roof? Only sixteen, she was. Tell George MacDonagh some of us haven't forgotten." She shuddered. Hearing the vile words coming out of her own mouth, she felt almost as if some demon had taken possession of her and was talking through her.

"I don't understand," George declared. "Why didn't you tell me? Why didn't you wake me up and tell me? Didn't you realize then that the production might be in jeopardy?"

"I suppose I did, but . . . truth?"

"Truth."

"I was afraid to hear whatever it was you might tell me," Maggie said. "Everywhere I turned, it seemed, there was George and this woman, George

and that woman. Nora was safe in the past,
but...sixteen! I couldn't handle it. I couldn't handle
having my worst suspicions about you confirmed."

George gave a strange, dark laugh. "In a way that's
marvelous to hear," he said wearily.

"It is?"

"More concerned with your feelings about me than
with the production. I wouldn't have dared hope for
that a day ago. And now how do you feel?"

"About what?"

"Can you stand to have your worst suspicions about
me confirmed?" Again the harsh laughter rang out
through the shadows. "But I suppose it doesn't really
matter, does it? Seeing as how you've declined to
marry me?"

"George, you don't understand at all. That has
nothing to do with you, it has to do with me."

He freed his arm from her grasp. "Phrase it any
way you want. Rejection is rejection."

"But I—"

"You know what the saddest word in the language
is, Emerald Eyes? 'But.' There's the car. Do me a
great kindness, will you? Ride in the back with Kathleen?"

"But—"

"There you go again. Hello, ladies," he said, as
they caught up with Kathleen and Genevieve. "From
the looks on your faces, you're going to make diabetes
the funnest thing since sliced bread. Do my eyes de-
ceive me, or do I see the first streaks of dawn?"

"Darling director," Genevieve began, "I'm going
to look like hell for the camera tomorrow. Bags *this*
big under my eyes."

"Good. You'll look like you wept through the night
for your poor lost Art. Keep me company up front.
Maggie said she wanted to stretch out in the back and
sleep. Everybody set, then?"

chapter 18

"MAGGIE! MAGGIE!"

She opened her eyes to the blazing light of day.

"Maggie?" It was Shelagh's voice, sounding so urgent that Maggie came to all at once. Her first thought was that Tom had taken a turn for the worse. "Come in," she called. "It's unlocked."

The four year old burst into the room. Her face was radiant with happiness. In her hands she cupped a tiny orange kitten, not much more substantial looking than a handful of cotton puffs. "Marmalade!" She ran across to Maggie's bed with her treasure. "Mrs. Durcan brought her this morning because she's done with nursing and everyone thought Denny and I had better have a present to cheer us up because Grandpop is in the hospital." Suddenly her eyes were solemn saucers. "He got sick last night, but he's on the mend now. Isn't that grand?"

"Indeed it is," Maggie said gently. She reached over to pat the trembling little kitten. It gave a tiny mew. Suddenly something broke inside Maggie. Tears came flooding down her face. "Shelagh, darling, I'm sorry, so silly—" She reached for a box of tissues at her bedside and began to mop at her eyes. "Sit down," she sniffled, patting her bed. "I have to ask you something. If I have a baby some day, a little girl, is it all right with you if I call her Shelagh?"

"That would be ever so grand." Shelagh clapped her hands. "May I be the godmother, then?"

"I'd be thrilled."

"But I don't know if I can go to the States for the christening," Shelagh sighed. "Air tickets are ever so dear." She looked stricken.

"I'll tell you what," Maggie said. "I'll bring the baby to Castlecove, and we'll have the christening at the church up in Leap. How's that?"

"Lovelier and lovelier! And my mama and papa can make the party here afterwards." She scrambled down off the bed, her new kitten all but forgotten. "I must go tell them."

"Whoa!" Maggie reached out and pulled the little girl back. "There's been enough confusion around here without *that* mix-up. We're talking about the future, you see. I'm not quite ready to have my baby. I'm not even married! So it's our secret. Not a word to anyone for now. All right?"

"Not even Maggie Durcan? She's my best friend. She loves babies."

"Not even Maggie Durcan. Promise?"

"I promise," Shelagh said solemnly. She held Marmalade next to her cheek. "I swear by Marmalade. I won't tell anyone."

"I can't ask for more than that."

"Shelagh!" Denny's thin voice came piping their way. "It's my turn with Marmalade. Shelagh? Where are you?"

Shelagh looked at Maggie and made a moue. "Men!" she sniffed, leaving Maggie collapsed in laughter on her pillow as child and kitten scampered from the room.

A moment later Shelagh returned on her own. "I found it!" she cried triumphantly.

"Found what?"

"My barette."

"What barette, pumpkin?"

"I thought I lost it in here, you see," the child said, "and when you were in Shanagarry George said he was sure you wouldn't mind if I looked, and it's a good thing I looked because I found that important paper that fell in the wastebasket by mistake and George said he would give it to you and you'd be ever so glad, only then it turned out my barette was in Denny's caboose, isn't that silly?"

"Very silly," Maggie agreed. "I'm glad you found it, anyway. And thank you for saving my important paper. That was very clever of you."

"I knew it was important because it didn't have any cross-outs on it."

After she had gone Maggie thought that maybe if she lay in that bed long enough, the entire mystery of the universe would unravel before her eyes. She traced a gentle circle on her abdomen. She thought about P. S. 41, just around the corner from her apartment, and the way the children shouted their exuberance at the end of the schoolday. She mentally dug up the lettuce in her garden and planted nutrient-rich spinach in its place. Or had she read somewhere that pediatricians no longer approved of spinach? She put the lettuce back.

No new annunciations were forthcoming, so Maggie got up, took a quick bath, and got dressed. She supposed that George and Adam, Genevieve and Candy and probably Larry were over at Castle Killashee, filming. She'd have a cup of tea and see if there was a car she could borrow. She had to see George, and she had to see him now.

Downstairs she got tea, along with a jug of creamy milk, from Bryan's shy helper, Colleen Quinn, who told her that George had put off shooting until the afternoon because Tom had summoned him to his hospital bedside.

"Summoned him?"

"All I know is," Colleen said shyly, "he talked to Kathleen, Tom did, and then Kathleen told George Tom wanted to see him, and off they went."

Maggie paced the drawing room. She went out to Kathleen's garden and weeded it clean, and only wished there were more weeds to pull. She went up to her room and changed her violet turtleneck sweater for a green plaid wool shirt, then changed back into the turtleneck, then put on her favorite sea green silk shirt, rolled up the sleeves, and tried to go to work.

She couldn't. Wasn't capable of so much as typing a laundry list.

She went searching for chitchat, a game of gin, any distraction, only to discover that the rest of the *Art O'Leary* company had decided to take advantage of the free morning to walk down to the harbor with Bryan and the kids to look into the possibility of chartering a sailboat for a jaunt to Clear Island, where the palm trees grew.

Then, at last, when she thought her expiration was imminent, she heard the sound of Tom Farley's Mercedes pulling off the road in front of the inn, and she saw George and Kathleen emerge. One look at their faces told her that, whatever urgency had impelled their visit to Tom's bedside, it was a happy urgency.

Once again Maggie and George confronted each other with a flight of stairs between them, only this time he was at the bottom looking up and she was at the top looking down.

His eyes had a kind of clarity to them that made his previous states of exuberance look like mere dress-rehearsals.

"That's a gorgeous shirt, Emerald Eyes," he started with teasing slowness, as though to tell her he knew they had an eternity before them. "Wearing the green, eh? You'll be growing shamrocks and singing 'Danny Boy' before you know it."

She smiled. It took all her strength to keep from rushing down the stairs into his arms, but something told her she mustn't, not quite yet. "Tom's doing well?" she asked.

"Beautifully. When we told him Genevieve would be paying a private call on him later today, the only thing on his mind was could he persuade his barber to come over to the hospital and give him a shave and a haircut before she arrived. Well," he added, "that wasn't quite the only thing on his mind."

"Oh?"

"He said he knew he was likely to go on for another thirty years but, still, being struck down the way he was last night made him feel he had to unburden himself of a secret he'd carried ever since Máire's death. Maggie—"

"It's all right, darling. I can take it. I can take anything. It's about Nora, isn't it?"

"Yes."

"You had an affair with her?"

"I know it seems shocking, a girl only sixteen, but I had just turned nineteen, and the truth of it was, I was the virgin, and she was the experienced one. Very experienced. Only I didn't know. I thought . . . forgive me, Maggie . . . I thought it was love. And, God help me, I suppose I loved the feeling of sinfulness about it, sneaking around, desperate lest anyone found out. When I was leaving for Dublin— This is very, very hard, Maggie."

"I love you, George. Nothing you can say will change that. Say everything that has to be said and let's get it behind us."

The dark-haired director drew a deep breath. "When I was getting ready to go to Dublin, to do my year at Trinity College, she said I had to take her with me. I'd ruined her, she claimed, and no Irishman would have her, and I had to pay up or she'd make such trouble I'd be forced to leave the country, if indeed I could get out of it alive. I took her with me. I detested her by that time, but I offered to marry her. It seemed only right. The night before we were going to wed, she got herself picked up by a couple of Brazilian playboys, and decided life with them looked like a more amusing bet."

"Dublin Dreams," Maggie breathed.

"Give the lady a cigar. Her father hated me first of all for 'ruining' her, and second of all for turning my pain and guilt and confusion into a movie. You can imagine how he felt when I came back here to make another movie. What a fool I was, thinking he'd have come to some kind of peace with himself and the world a decade later."

"But I don't understand," Maggie said. "Didn't he know what she was? A parent may love a child no matter how dreadful its faults, but not to see the faults—"

"You've seen Liam Keaveny. Poor sad man that he is. His wife died when Nora was a tot. I suppose he did the best he could, or thought he did, anyway. To admit, even to himself, that she was what she was would have been, I think, to die."

"And Tom's secret?" Maggie asked.

"Even when Nora ran off with those two men, I still didn't understand. I thought I'd destroyed her, that I had failed her. I never realized that she'd looked on me as nothing but a ticket out of Castlecove. When Máire, that blessed woman, saw *Dublin Dreams,* she understood my pain. She wrote me a letter, telling me that Nora had had a deep need for love that she tried to fulfill through sex and I had to stop hating myself for what Nora had been and done. The fault was her own, Máire said, for taking Nora on as a helper, thinking she could reform the girl by giving her a mother's love, when so clearly the problem was much more complicated."

Maggie clung to the banister. "She *was* the guilty one, letting you go off with Nora thinking what you thought."

"No." George shook his head. "She had to go on living here. She had to bring up her own daughter here. She had to face Liam Keaveny every evening at five-fifteen. She was right to sacrifice me. And when she saw *Dublin Dreams* and realized how shattered I was, she did write that letter. And, as she lay on her deathbed, she gave it to Tom to mail for her."

"Oh," Maggie breathed. "And he didn't?"

"He did. He sent it to Dublin, my last known address, with instructions to forward. But by then I was six or seven addresses removed, and the letter never reached me. He told me tonight that he'd always suspected as much, but he'd let the matter drift because he'd figured Castlecove and Nora were long gone from my mind, and why stir up misery? When the trouble happened on the set, he suspected Liam was behind it. When I told him at the hospital about the midnight phone call, that confirmed his fears. He's talking to Liam now."

"That poor man!" Maggie said, suddenly pitying Liam for having to confront the sad truth.

"Tom said he's known about her for a while. Truth always comes out, doesn't it? That's why Tom was angry at Liam. He knew the man was stirring up this hatred against me in a futile attempt to rehabilitate Nora in his own and the public's eyes. But Tom will be gentle. I bet Liam's back on his bar stool tonight. Your thugs, by the way, weren't locals...a trio of roadworkers from Dunmanway Liam used to work with. Liam took a cue from our talk with Kathleen in the pub, and told them we were crass Americans bent on spoiling an Irish treasure. Emerald Eyes? Are we going to stand here like this for the next hundred years? Either you're coming down the stairs, or I'm coming up."

"There are advantages either way, when you think about it," Maggie said conversationally. "If I come down, we could go have a Guinness in the pub. I'm all but parched to death, hearing you talk so much. Then again, if you come up, we could go to my room. I might even be talked into locking my door, for once."

As she turned the key behind her, Maggie said to George, "Please don't look at me that way."

Her tall, dark-haired lover sank down on her bed. "Whatever do you mean? Don't tell me you brought me up here to discuss camera angles."

"You said your piece, and now I'm going to say mine." Maggie sat next to George and took one of his hands in both hers. "I meant it, you see, when I told you that my not wanting to marry you had nothing to do with *you*, not with the women, or anything else—"

"Emerald Eyes," George groaned, covering his face with his hands, "I can't bear it. Did I go through all that only to hear you tell me I still don't have you?"

"—because," Maggie went on blithely, "it had to do with *me*. I thought I wasn't meant for marriage, you see. When I was in college, and John was my professor, our affair was very exciting—"

"Thanks." George grimaced.

"—only when we got married it stopped being exciting, and I always thought it was marriage itself that had killed our passion. I decided I would never marry again, not even if I fell in love again. But this morning, when Shelagh and I were discussing our baby—"

"Do we have a baby?" George asked. "How clever of us. I adore babies. Only I didn't think—"

Maggie fell backwards onto the bed. "Oh, George, George," she sputtered, "I do love you so very, awfully, madly much."

"Does all this mean you'll marry me, then?" He leaned over her. He stroked her cheeks in that way of his. "I think it would be nicer for the baby, don't you?"

"You truly want children?" Maggie's eyes fixed themselves hungrily on his cheekbones, his dimpled chin, his ever-changing mouth. "You don't mind if I have two or three between the films I write for you?"

"How about writing films for me between the two or three babies?"

His hands went to her hair. He kissed her eyebrows, her nose, the corners of her mouth.

"You're not allergic to cats, are you?" she murmured.

He kissed her throat. "No allergies at all. You don't mind if we spend some time in California as well as New York and Castlecove and parts unknown?"

"It's the best place for growing avocados," Maggie said, "and I have always wanted to grow avocados. May I go on drinking beer in public?"

"May I go on kissing you in private?"

The words stopped. Their bodies strained toward each other. Their clothes became a heap on the floor. Their breath was one breath, their heartbeat a single pulse, their desire the cosmic dance itself.

A while later George said, "I could begin to believe you like me a little."

"I hope you're not entirely convinced," Maggie murmured, with infinite tenderness.

"Oh?"

"I mean," she said, "I'd like to have to state my case again."

"Before lunch?" George asked.

She pretended to consider. "I've been thinking it wouldn't hurt me to skip a meal. My jeans are getting tight."

"You're perfect the way you are, but you know what?" His finger trailed across her breasts and belly. "I just lost my appetite. For lunch, I mean."

chapter 19

Castlecove, County Cork, Ireland. For immediate release.

George MacDonagh today wound up filming on his major new production, Lament for Art O'Leary.

The film, based on an eighteenth-century poem by Corkwoman Eileen O'Leary, stars Genevieve Joyce as the poet, and MacDonagh in the title role, his first appearance in front of the camera.

Among the many unique characteristics of the production was the use of local non-professional actors in all but the two starring roles. Syndicated movie reviewer Lorenzo F. X. Delgado has predicted, in a copyrighted article appearing in more than two hundred papers, that retired roadworker Liam Keaveny of Leap will win an Oscar for best supporting actor for his role of the villainous Abraham Morris, the British soldier who shot Art O'Leary because he coveted his horse.

Photographed entirely on videotape at Castle Killashee by cinematographer Adam Manski and technical assistant Candace Kinicott, Art O'Leary will be edited by MacDonagh in New York and transferred to 35-millimeter film. Distribution is set for next spring, following a gala Saint Patrick's Day opening in Boston, hometown of the director's wife.

There's nothing more precious than your

Second Chance at Love
™

_____ 05703-7 **FLAMENCO NIGHTS #1** Susanna Collins

_____ 05637-5 **WINTER LOVE SONG #2**
Meredith Kingston

_____ 05624-3 **THE CHADBOURNE LUCK #3**
Lucia Curzon

_____ 05777-0 **OUT OF A DREAM #4** Jennifer Rose

_____ 05878-5 **GLITTER GIRL #5** Jocelyn Day

_____ 05863-7 **AN ARTFUL LADY #6** Sabina Clark

_____ 05694-4 **EMERALD BAY #7** Winter Ames

_____ 05776-2 **RAPTURE REGAINED #8**
Serena Alexander

_____ 05801-7 **THE CAUTIOUS HEART #9**
Philippa Heywood

_____ 05907-2 **ALOHA YESTERDAY #10**
Meredith Kingston

_____ 05638-3 **MOONFIRE MELODY #11** Lily Bradford

_____ 06132-8 **MEETING WITH THE PAST #12**
Caroline Halter

All of the above titles are $1.75 per copy

Second Chance at Love

™

____ 05623-5 **WINDS OF MORNING #13** Laurie Marath

____ 05704-5 **HARD TO HANDLE #14** Susanna Collins

____ 06067-4 **BELOVED PIRATE #15** Margie Michaels

____ 05978-1 **PASSION'S FLIGHT #16** Marilyn Mathieu

____ 05847-5 **HEART OF THE GLEN #17** Lily Bradford

____ 05977-3 **BIRD OF PARADISE #18** Winter Ames

____ 05705-3 **DESTINY'S SPELL #19** Susanna Collins

____ 06106-9 **GENTLE TORMENT #20** Johanna Phillips

____ 06059-3 **MAYAN ENCHANTMENT #21** Lila Ford

____ 06301-0 **LED INTO SUNLIGHT #22** Claire Evans

____ 06131-X **CRYSTAL FIRE #23** Valerie Nye

____ 06150-6 **PASSION'S GAMES #24**
Meredith Kingston

____ 06160-3 **GIFT OF ORCHIDS #25** Patti Moore

____ 06108-5 **SILKEN CARESSES #26** Samantha Carroll

____ 06318-5 **SAPPHIRE ISLAND #27** Diane Crawford

All of the above titles are $1.75 per copy

Available at your local bookstore or return this form to:

SECOND CHANCE AT LOVE
The Berkley/Jove Publishing Group
200 Madison Avenue, New York, New York 10016

Please enclose 50¢ for postage and handling for one book, 25¢ each add'l book ($1.25 max.). No cash, CODs or stamps. Total amount enclosed: $_____ in check or money order.

NAME_____

ADDRESS_____

CITY_____ STATE/ZIP_____

Allow six weeks for delivery.   SK-41

**WATCH FOR
6 NEW TITLES EVERY MONTH!**

™

Second Chance at Love

™

____	06335-5	**APHRODITE'S LEGEND #28**	Lynn Fairfax
____	06336-3	**TENDER TRIUMPH #29**	Jasmine Craig
____	06280-4	**AMBER-EYED MAN #30**	Johanna Phillips
____	06249-9	**SUMMER LACE #31**	Jenny Nolan
____	06305-3	**HEARTTHROB #32**	Margarett McKean
____	05626-X	**AN ADVERSE ALLIANCE #33**	Lucia Curzon
____	06162-X	**LURED INTO DAWN #34**	Catherine Mills
____	06195-6	**SHAMROCK SEASON #35**	Jennifer Rose
____	06304-5	**HOLD FAST TIL MORNING #36**	Beth Brookes
____	06282-0	**HEARTLAND #37**	Lynn Fairfax
____	06408-4	**FROM THIS DAY FORWARD #38**	Jolene Adams
____	05968-4	**THE WIDOW OF BATH #39**	Anne Devon

All titles $1.75

Available at your local bookstore or return this form to:

SECOND CHANCE AT LOVE
The Berkley/Jove Publishing Group
200 Madison Avenue, New York, New York 10016

**Please enclose 50¢ for postage and handling for one book, 25¢
each add'l book ($1.25 max.). No cash, CODs or stamps. Total
amount enclosed: $ _____ in check or money order.**

NAME_____

ADDRESS_____

CITY_____ STATE/ZIP_____

Allow six weeks for delivery.   SK-41